It wouldn't be so bad if her body didn't react every time she set eyes on him.

She'd never been an overly sensitive person—not in a sexual or sensual way. Yet now it seemed as if her skin had been flayed by the Outback dust, exposing nerve-endings that leapt and tweaked and tingled whenever the handsome vet appeared.

With a sigh that made her windscreen mist over, she started the car and headed back towards the hospital, determined in some way to inoculate herself against the man's potent attraction. Arriving home to a phone call from Philip helped, but unfortunately she'd no sooner hung up than Tom appeared.

'I promised Carrie that if she held off publishing a story now, we'd give her an exclusive for the wedding. I said we'd already fixed a date—the first of January. That okay with you?'

Anna stared at him.

'But we're not getting married,' she reminded him.

Dear Reader

Doctors in the Outback, this series of four books set in the Australian Outback, of which OUTBACK ENGAGEMENT is the first, was prompted by a big change in my own life. My husband and I shifted from a house on the very edge of Australia, overlooking a broad stretch of water that feeds in from the Pacific Ocean, to a small cottage in a small outback town (population about 2,500) in Central Queensland. From the beach to the bush—that's an Aussie word for anywhere that isn't in a city.

After the rush and bustle of the tourist-oriented city where we lived before, the relaxed pace of the Outback really suits us. Where before we had jet-skis roaring past as we ate breakfast on the front deck, now we have a large and very quiet kangaroo occasionally popping in to feed on our well-watered back lawn, and the most dominant noise is birdsong.

I am really enjoying my new life in the Outback, and I hope these books will bring you a taste of it—a taste of the variety of life in the bush, the highs and lows, the tears and laughter, and, of course, the love those that live out here seek and find.

With best wishes

Meredith Webber

OUTBACK
ENGAGEMENT

BY
MEREDITH WEBBER

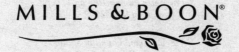

All the characters in this book have no existence outside the imagination of the author, and have no relation whatsoever to anyone bearing the same name or names. They are not even distantly inspired by any individual known or unknown to the author, and all the incidents are pure invention.

First published in Great Britain 2003
Harlequin Mills & Boon Limited,
Eton House, 18-24 Paradise Road, Richmond, Surrey TW9 1SR

© Meredith Webber 2003

ISBN 0 263 83478 6

Set in Times Roman 10½ on 11¼ pt.
03-1103-53042

Printed and bound in Spain
by Litografia Rosés, S.A., Barcelona

PROLOGUE

July 23rd
Dear Editor,
I enjoyed your story on lonely country bachelors seeking women to share their lives, but in my opinion you missed the best of them, my stepson, Tom. He lost his mother when he was three, and he was brought up by his father until I came into their lives when he was eight. His father and I had twelve glorious years—the men in that family are real *men—and two lovely daughters together before my husband was tragically killed in a small plane crash.*

Tom, at twenty, took over the role of man of the house, and for ten years was both father and brother to his half-sisters who were six and two at the time of their father's death. He was only freed of this role when I remarried a year ago, when he was able to follow his heart, return to the country and set up as a vet in a small outback town. His fiancée, however, was a city girl, and refused to go with him.

But if there are women out there looking for a kind, considerate, caring, outback man, they couldn't go further than our Tom.

Part of an email from Tom Fleming to Grace Winthrop:

August 6th
Thanks for your email, Grace, it was good to hear from

you. Yes, life back where I feel I belong in the country is really suiting me, and I know you won't take it the wrong way when I say that I am really enjoying my bachelor existence. Of course, I miss what you and I had, but after all those years as the only male in a houseful of women, to be women-free is wonderful. Obviously, this won't last, but I don't think the novelty will wear off for a year or two at least. I can use the inside bathroom without dodging drying stockings or underwear, my razor is never clogged with leg hair, I can leave my dirty dishes in the sink all day, and only dust when I can actually write my name in what's settled on the top of furniture. Not to mention eating steak and chips every night for dinner. Slobbish, I know, but I feel it's my life at last.

Great to hear your job is going well…

Email from Sally Warburton to sister Grace:

August 8th
Hi, Gracie,
I know you said lover-boy was safe from predatory women for the near future and you intended leaving him alone out there until he came to his senses, but have you seen this week's Women! *mag? Letters to the editor on Page 37!*
Sally

Memo from Grace Warburton to her boss, Mark Collins:

August 9th
Mark, I know it's short notice, but I'd like to take unpaid leave for six weeks, starting whenever you can find someone to fill in for me, but preferably from the end of the month. The matter is personal and urgent.

Memo from Editor, *Women!* magazine to Carrie Kilmer, ace reporter:

September 2nd
Carrie, attached is letter from doting stepmother.
Trouble is I printed it a few weeks ago and have already
had more replies to it than we had to the article we ran
on country bachelors. Have forwarded on letters to
'Tom' via the stepmother's address, but feel someone
should get out to his outback hide-away, sleuths tell me
it's a town called Merriwee, and interview him. Get
photos with animals, the cuter the better. Think of the
scoop if we can marry off this man. Have booked you
on flight to nearest town with regular air service on
Saturday 9th September. Ticket confirmation also at-
tached.

Email from Penelope Fleming to sister Patience, now in
residence at women's college at university:

September 6th
Hi, Patience,
*   You wouldn't believe the bags of letters Mum has sent*
on to Tom! All from women wanting to marry him. How
Mum could have written that letter, I can't imagine, but
apparently she did it because she thinks he's lonely. You
know what Mum's like about love and marriage—to her
it's the ultimate turn-on—and she wants Tom to expe-
rience it. He's going to be absolutely besieged *and you*
know how impossible he is at choosing women.
Remember Anthea, the one before Ghastly Grace? The
one who insisted he buy an Armani suit? Poor Tom! He
hated it, but he's so hopeless at saying no to women. I
know it was Grace who proposed—I heard her. It was
just sheer luck GG got the promotion at work so decided
she couldn't possibly move to the country. Not that she

told Tom that was the reason—all she went on about were her allergies and how living in the country was impossible for her.

Anyway, I think someone's got to get out there to back him up and check out any of these women who might actually turn up. Actually, I have to go because you can't leave uni and I've got nothing much on at school which is boring anyway. I know you'll try to argue so I went ahead and booked a plane ticket over the internet.

But could you come home on Friday, then we can say we're going shopping on Saturday morning. That way, you can drive me to the airport and then, once I'm on the plane, you can phone Tom and explain to Mum. You can say I was so unhappy at school I just had to go up and see him. And once I'm there I know I can persuade him to let me stay a month, then it will be school holidays, and you and Mum will be coming up. If I haven't sorted things out by then, we'll have to give up!

Email from Anna Talbot to fiancé Philip Ducartes:

September 7th
So, darling, I'm settled into my 'outback' town, and still very grateful that you understood how much it meant to me to come here. Only problem is with the cat I adopted while in Melbourne. It's obviously a city cat and hates the country, refusing to get out of its travelling cage. I've tried everything I know, and so tomorrow, before I begin work, I shall have to find a vet...

The rest of the email was personal.

CHAPTER ONE

ANNA looked around the small living room and gave a satisfied nod. The framed prints of colourful reef fish, lurking in vivid coral gardens, brightened the walls of the room, and the rug she'd thrown over the tired-looking beige lounge exactly matched the blue of the water in the pictures.

Photos of her parents, and the animals she'd left behind—Kurt, the Doberman, Fancy, the cat, and Streak, her beloved though now aging Arabian horse—were clustered on top of the television. On the middle of the small round dining table she'd set an oblong mat, cross-stitched by her mother, and on it a brilliant blue vase she'd found in a second-hand stall during a prowl around the markets in Melbourne.

As the yard around her small, government-provided house was bare of grass and lacking a garden, she'd picked some sprays of eucalyptus leaves from the lower branch of a tree that stood halfway between the house and the hospital. The scent of the leaves reminded her of home, and added the final touch of 'homeliness' to her new abode.

'Now all I have to do is sort you out,' she said, walking into the tiny kitchen, which opened off the dining area, and addressing a wire-topped animal carrier.

The cat crouched in one corner of the open container and glared balefully up at her.

'Come on, you've got to eat,' Anna coaxed. 'And there must be other things that need attending to, so how about you get out of that box and take a look around the house?

I've put your litter tray in the bathroom so you don't have to venture outdoors.'

The cat narrowed its vivid blue eyes to threatening slits and growled.

Anna sighed. She'd missed her animals so much during the weeks she'd spent in Melbourne that she'd been happy to accept custody of Cassie, the cat of a friend who was going back to South Africa. And she'd imagined, over the next few weeks while she'd applied for jobs and waited for interview appointments, that she and the cat had bonded—as much as one could ever bond with an independent-minded Siamese.

The three-day journey north to central Queensland had taught her differently. Cass hadn't minded the car—in fact, she'd often travelled in it around the city, sitting up behind the back seat like a car ornament. However, it had soon become apparent she was a city cat. The great outdoors terrified her to such an extent she'd yowled and pulled against the lead she'd been trained to wear whenever Anna had tried to tempt her out of the car for a comfort stop or to stay overnight in a motel.

'Your ancestors probably prowled the jungles of South-East Asia,' Anna told the belligerent animal. 'And look at you, cowering in your box like someone who's never seen the outside of a city apartment.'

The slitted eyes blinked slowly, and the proudly tilted head and steely stare conveyed the message that Cass's ancestors had been the darlings of a royal court, not jungle marauders.

'OK, stay there! I've only got two more days before I start work, and I'm not going to spend them persuading you out of that box. I'm going for a walk uptown.'

It was stupid, talking to a cat, but as Anna had driven north through the vast empty stretches of inland Australia, she'd begun to share just a little of the cat's apprehension. What had seemed like the ultimate adventure, to practise medicine in an Australian outback town, had become just a tiny bit scary for a woman born and bred in the city. It wasn't that South Africa didn't have a lot of outback-type country of its own, it was just that she hadn't ever experienced it.

Now all the emptiness through which she'd travelled had seemed to magnify the distance she'd already come from her home in order to fulfil a long-held dream.

Six months…

'No, I'm from Durban,' she'd explained to Elizabeth Foster, the head of the hospital's clerical staff, who'd welcomed her to Merriwee the previous afternoon then shown her over the hospital, introducing her to staff on duty then taking her across to the house.

But though Anna had drawn a rough map of her country and had pointed out exactly where Durban was, she was left with the impression that Elizabeth still believed there were only two cities in South Africa—Johannesburg and Cape Town.

'Well, my own ignorance of Australia was just as bad when I arrived,' Anna admitted, still addressing the unresponsive cat because there was no one else to listen to her conversation.

Then she shook her head at her own behaviour and, grabbing a wide-brimmed straw hat from the hook by the kitchen door, took herself off to explore the town.

From what she'd seen on her first exploratory foray to the supermarket, Merriwee was divided into two parts by a railway line. The hospital was on the outskirts of the second, mainly residential section, while the shops and presumably the local council and business offices were across the tracks.

Am I on the right side or the wrong side? she wondered as she strode past the hospital and up the long drive. The roads were paved, but the footpaths were for the most part stony, weed-infested strips of ground, inviting an unwary walker to turn an ankle. Anna stuck to the road. After all, the traffic was practically non-existent.

She reached the main road through the town and turned left, walking towards the railway line. About to cross it—she'd never seen a train in the town so that wasn't a problem—she noticed a sign she hadn't seen before. White writing on a blue background proclaimed VET'S SURGERY. The sign pointed down another side street—this one running parallel with the railway line.

Pity for the anxious and upset animal she'd inherited made her turn that way, following the road past the end of the railway line to a fence, though a cattle grid and a gravel track with a cluster of trees at the end of it suggested there might be a house—and presumably a vet's surgery—hidden from view. She picked her way cautiously across the grid, not wanting to end up in her own hospital with a broken leg, and followed the track, smiling to herself as she realised she'd walked a long way around to get to a place that was virtually next door to her new home.

Although it was late afternoon, the sun was still hot so the trees, when she reached them, provided welcome shade. They were planted closely, a mix of native eucalypts and shade trees familiar from home, jacarandas, poinciana, and broad-leafed figs. The result was an area of dense shade which grew denser as she walked on so the house, when she finally saw it, seemed in danger of being swallowed up by the vegetation.

But the wide stoep—no, she'd have to learn to call it a veranda—would be cool, she realised, and the house would be well protected from winter winds.

She looked around and saw a smaller building to the right of the house, and, guessing it would be the surgery, headed that way. It was locked, though the small sign on the door stating surgery hours—4 p.m. to 6 p.m. Monday to Friday—suggested it should be open.

Anna knew it was Friday and was reasonably sure of the time, but she checked her watch automatically. Four-thirty. It should definitely be open.

There was no mention of weekend surgery hours so, anxious about the cat, she walked around to the back of the building, hoping to find someone she could speak to.

A row of small, wired runs with neat brick enclosures along one end suggested the vet might hospitalise his or her patients. Anna continued walking, peering into the long cage-like structures, pausing to talk quietly to a tired-looking German shepherd who lay, anxiously studying his plastered leg, in the doorway of his sheltered area.

The dog failed to respond, and Anna moved on, then backtracked as she saw a movement behind the dog.

'Hey! Are you hiding in there?' she called to the figure she could just discern, crouched in the enclosed space behind the dog.

'As a matter of fact, I am,' a curt voice replied. 'So why don't you take the hint and leave?'

Shocked by such rudeness in a country where she'd met with nothing but kindness, Anna stood her ground, peering through the wire to see if she could see more of the man who'd spoken.

'But I need to talk to the vet,' she said. 'I've got this paranoid cat and haven't a clue how to handle her.'

'You've got a what?' the voice said, then there was a shuffle of movement, the sound of a gate creaking open and the figure of a man—so tall he must have been terribly cramped in his hiding place—rose up on the far side of another wire-netting barrier. 'What are you? English? Good grief, has Pat gone international now? Am I on the internet as well as Australia-wide?'

Anna squinted through the wire at the man, who was obviously mad. The run was about eight metres long, and he was through the wire at the other end. On the outside, as she was, but she measured the distance between them with her eyes and knew she'd have time to run away from him if he came towards her.

'I don't know what you're talking about, or who this Pat person is,' she said, 'but I'm not English. I'm South African. Or at least I think of myself that way because I grew up there, though I *was* born in England and—'

'Spare me!' the man muttered, putting his hand to his forehead as if her explanation—which he'd *asked* for, mind you—was the final straw in some immense disaster.

But his disaster was none of her business—the cat was.

'About my cat—are you the vet? If not, can you tell me where to find him? Or her?'

She spoke slowly and carefully in case the man had trouble understanding either her accent or simple English, but he ignored all but the least important part of what she'd said.

'Or her? This is large-animal territory, lady. The big Brahman cattle around here would knock over most of the women vets I know. Quite a few of the men, too.'

Anna slid her fingers into the wire of the cage, gripping it as if by finger pressure alone she could hold onto her temper. The man on the further side of the run looked normal enough—in fact, even through two lots of wire, he was remarkably good-looking. And he had a voice like peanut chocolate—smooth and rich but with something satisfyingly crunchy in it. Not that looks or peanut-chocolaty voices were any measure of mental ability or sanity.

'I do not need someone to look at my Brahman cattle,' she said firmly, after reminding herself that Philip also had a very pleasant voice—and he was *very* good-looking!—'but at my cat.'

'Do you have Brahman cattle?'

The man at the far end of the run sounded almost interested, though there was a silkiness in the seductive voice which she automatically mistrusted.

'Of course I don't have Brahman cattle. What do you think? I'm on a working holiday in Australia with my herd of Brahman cattle?'

'No, but you could have bought some as an excuse. I wouldn't have put it past a determined woman to do just that.'

This weird retort seemed to confirm that he was mad, but the conversation was peculiar enough—and personal enough now he was denigrating the female of the species—for her to pursue it.

'Why would a determined woman buy Brahman cattle?' she asked, pressing her face closer to the wire as if a better view of the man might help her understand what was happening.

'Same reason they'd buy a cat!' the man said triumphantly. 'Because they read that stupid letter in the stupid magazine and thought the way to a vet's heart was through animals. Well, you're far too late, lady! I've been pursued by women with basset hounds, budgerigars and probably pet beetles if the truth be known, but I am *not* in the market for a wife—understand?'

He threw his arms in the air, muttered, 'Women!' in a tone of utter loathing and turned from her, walking not around the cages towards Anna but away, so his figure grew smaller, and smaller and…

She'd better go after him before he disappeared altogether. He might be mad, but he was also, apparently, the vet, and a mad vet was better than no vet at all when one had a paranoid cat.

Hurrying around the end of the cages, Anna caught sight of him opening a gate into a small yard. Two goats greeted him with loud bleats of delight—or perhaps hunger—and distracted him sufficiently for Anna to reach the post-and-rail fence without him realising she'd followed.

'About my cat,' she began, and smiled to herself as her voice jolted him into a startled yelp. He spun around, step-

ping backwards when he saw her so close, and catching
the heel of one elastic-sided boot on the animals' water
trough. Down he went in a tangle of long limbs and over-
excited goat, crashing to the ground with a string of oaths
which should have turned the air blue.

Knowing she was at least partly responsible for his accident didn't stop Anna laughing. In fact, he looked so
funny she was still smothering giggles when she slipped
through the fence and finally reached him.

'Here, take my hand. See if you can stand up,' she said,
pushing off one goat with her right hand and holding out
her left hand towards the fallen man.

He gave her a look of intense dislike and managed to
struggle to his feet unaided, then, bent double because he'd
fallen inside the goats' shelter, he moved cautiously out
into the open. The spilt water had muddied his tan mole-
skins and his faded blue shirt, and his sense of humour—
if he had one—was obviously not working, but to Anna's
professional eyes he looked OK.

To her personal eyes, he looked more than OK—an *ex-
ceptionally* attractive man if you fancied dark, rugged good
looks. She reminded herself she didn't—that fair-haired
men were far more elegant. She touched her thumb to the
inner part of Philip's ring and silently excused herself for
thinking about another man's appearance. After all, a
woman would have to be dead *not* to notice this man. He
oozed masculinity in the same way roses gave off perfume,
without being consciously aware of the potency of that
sensory attraction.

Now, where had that thought come from?

Anxious to block any more such notions, Anna shifted
back to professional mode.

'Are you all right?'

He fired a look of scorn her way, from eyes so true a
blue she thought of cornflowers.

'No thanks to you,' he growled, running his hands over

his shirt. It was an ineffectual attempt to clean up as the mud spread further. But the movement attracted her eyes to the breadth of his chest within the shirt. 'What's with you, anyway?' He rubbed his hands together to try to rid them of the sticky mess, then wiped them on the turned-up cuffs of his long sleeves. 'Don't you understand no means no? Or don't South African women use that catch-cry?'

Now he was denigrating her country as well as women. Anna forgot the broad chest and sensory attraction, and drew herself up to her full one hundred and seventy-seven centimetres. Then she shot him some scorn of her own, though she wasn't sure her wishy-washy green eyes could produce as much of it as his blue ones had.

'I understand that you are the most insufferably rude man I have ever met. I've also gathered you have an unhealthy antipathy towards women and possibly some kind of persecution complex, but apparently you're also the vet and as I assume a town this size only has one such specialist, I have to put up with your peculiarities in order to get help for my cat.'

He blinked and the expression in the blue eyes shifted from suspicion to a wary kind of confusion.

'You really have a cat?'

Anna, who'd been temporarily distracted by the shifting expressions in the blue eyes, nodded then stepped backwards, exiting the yard, as the man came towards her.

'Do you think I made it up? That I travel around with an imaginary cat?' she snapped, aggravated with herself as well as him now, because the distraction disturbed her. 'Of course I've got a cat! Why else would I be here?'

'"Of course I've got a cat."' He mimicked her accent then added in his own Australian drawl, 'Though I can't see any sign of one. In Australia it's usual to bring the animal you want treated along with you when you come to the vet.'

Anna took a deep breath. He might be the best-looking man she'd seen yet, in this country of good-looking men, but he was also the most irritating man she'd ever met, here or at home. And he was making her madder than a mud wasp whose nest had been disturbed!

'I didn't bring the cat because I wasn't coming here. I was walking uptown when I saw your sign. And I wouldn't have brought the cat anyway—partly because it's advice I need but specifically because closing her back in the cage to carry her here might strengthen her psychological reliance on it.'

The blue eyes crinkled at the corners as he narrowed them into much the same suspicious stare Cass had used earlier.

'Your cat has a psychological reliance on a travelling cage?'

Disbelief curled around the words like smoke from a campfire, but Anna ignored it. She nodded agreement, then put it into words.

'She won't get out. I've tried tempting her with every treat I can think of, including fried bacon which she usually loves. I've tried shifting her food and water dishes further and further away from the cage, but she refuses to move.'

Disbelief still radiated from him in waves, but Anna sensed a smidgen of interest as well. She decided to push a little further.

'Nor will she use her litter tray and she's usually the most fastidious of cats.'

The man was frowning now, studying her and frowning, and from the way the frown lines were deepening he wasn't liking what he saw.

'Is she eating?'

'I told you, no.'

'Drinking?'

'A little milk.'

'How can she drink some milk without leaving her cage if you've put the dishes further away?'

He was being a pain, and standing far too close to her now he'd reached the yard rail and was leaning over it, so Anna glared at him.

'Because I pushed the milk and water dishes over near her again,' she said defiantly. 'I couldn't let her die of dehydration.'

'And what do you think I can do? I'm a vet, not a cat psychologist.'

'I would have thought your studies included some work on animal behaviours. In fact, I know they do. But for some reason, probably because I'm a woman and you're in dire need of psychological help yourself as far as dealing with my half of the human race goes, you're choosing not to help. Well, I happen to like that cat, and I'm not going to be put off getting help for her by some stubborn, boorish, misogynistic imbecile who hides from clients in a dog kennel.'

She thrust her hands on her hips and dared him to defy her again, but to her surprise he didn't argue.

In fact, he laughed.

'I hope you're not laughing at me.' She scowled to reiterate the message, but this new spurt of anger was caused by her own reaction to the laughter. It was a deep, belly-rumbling noise so joyous it made her want to join in. Perhaps because it reminded her of her Uncle Fred's laugh—a sound so filled with merriment and goodwill she'd rarely heard it without smiling.

This obstreperous stranger had no right to have Uncle Fred's laugh!

Though, in all fairness, she probably couldn't hold that against him. It wasn't as if he'd stolen it.

She was watching one of the goats making mud pies in the spilt water and mentally listing all the things she *could* hold against the man when he moved, opening the gate and sliding through before shutting it behind him. Then he reached out and took her hand—her left hand—lifting it so the sun flashed off the diamond on her ring finger.

'What's this? An engagement ring? Well, that's different. Though I guess it's actually a cubic zircona. Who could possibly afford a diamond the size of a fairly well-fed cattle tick?'

Anna snatched her hand away, but not before she registered the hard calluses on his palm against her own soft skin.

'A cattle tick? You're likening my diamond to a cattle tick? I'll have you know this is a top-quality, blue-white South African stone, of a purity rarely seen.'

She gave him yet another glare, though they seemed to bounce right off him, and added with a touch of her own belligerence, 'And the expression is "a diamond as big as the Ritz", not as big as a cattle tick!'

He laughed again, shook his head, then linked his arm through hers.

'Come on,' he said. 'Let's go visit your cat.'

Anna was at first startled by his familiarity—then even more shocked by her own reaction to it. The man's touch scorched her skin like a hot veld wind and she had to fight an urge to snatch her arm away and rub at it to erase the lingering heat.

Tom regretted touching her the moment he did it, but he could hardly push away from her now. The problem was, she'd reminded him of Penny—well, both his half-sisters would have stood toe to toe with him and argued as this woman had, but it was the younger, Penny, he missed most these days.

Because she made him laugh?

Probably.

Anyway, in that instant he'd done what he would have done with Pen—or Patience come to that. He'd linked his arm through his visitor's and guided her back around the surgery.

'Where's the cat? Do we need to drive?'

The woman solved the proximity problem, which, for all his current aggravation with women, was reminding his body that they had their uses. She moved away from him, peering around his yard as if trying to get her bearings.

'I can't see for the trees,' she said, 'but isn't the hospital just over there?' She waved her hand in roughly the right direction. 'I came down the road along the railway line, but surely there's a shorter way to get back.'

'The hospital? Why do you need to get to the hospital? Did you take the cat there?'

He stared at her, partly from surprise but also because she was a remarkably attractive woman—maybe even beautiful if he could see more of her face under the hat. Shorter men than he might quibble over her height, but he'd ricked his back kissing small women in the past so he saw height as an advantage. Not that he had any intention of kissing her, of course.

She was slender—probably spent half her life dieting— with long, long legs and long slim arms, attached to a body that curved in all the right places. And she looked about as at home in the country as a thoroughbred would look in a mob of wild brumbies. A slim miniskirt clung to her thighs, the stretchy top she wore ended just short enough to show a strip of tanned skin across her belly, while the silly footwear, platform thongs with a bright daisy between the big and second toes, would be covered in dust within a kilometre. That's if she didn't fall off them and break an ankle.

But by now, possibly because of his silence, she'd looked up at him, so he had a better view of the oval face, with all the features in perfect symmetry, though dominated by almond-shaped green eyes fringed with long, golden brown eyelashes and framed by well-arched brows.

Currently drawn together in a frown!

So, she probably wasn't studying him in the same assessing way he was studying her—or, if she was, she didn't fancy what she saw. Though his sisters claimed he was OK in the looks department—a bit rough but that wasn't a bad thing in a bloke, they said.

But the stranger was studying him more as if he were an exhibit in a zoo—*Homo sapiens* but with a query after it.

'Why would anyone take a cat to a hospital?' she finally asked, and he guessed she didn't really want an answer but had to verbalise her thoughts.

'You said the cat was there,' he reminded her.

She smiled and a lot of the antipathy he'd been feeling towards females dissolved in the warm radiance of that simple shift of full, ripe, red and, oh, so kissable lips.

Red alert! Red alert! That's how they get to you, his inner voice reminded him. They tempt you with their bodies, tantalise you with their lips, seduce you into thinking an affair is all they want, then suddenly you're engaged to be married and not sure it's quite what you wanted...

Though surely with Grace it had been what he wanted. Marriage, a family, kids...

'The cat's there because it's where we're going to be living, she and I. I'm the new doctor. Anna Talbot.'

She held out her hand—not the one with the huge diamond on it—and in spite of new 'red alert' warnings clanging in Tom's head he took it, shook it, then had trouble letting go.

'The new doctor, eh?' His gaze skimmed down her scantily clad figure. 'Well, you sure should liven up the town.'

He grinned then saw the panic in her eyes, and instantly regretted his smart remark.

'You're teasing me. I'm dressed all wrong, aren't I? I wondered when I shopped the other day and everyone was nice, but they kept sneaking looks at me. But friends in Melbourne kept telling me how hot Merriwee would be. They said to take cool clothes…'

'My sisters would think your outfit *very* cool,' Tom assured her, giving the warm, soft digits he was still holding a reassuring squeeze. 'And the town could do with a shake-up so dress any way you like. I'm Tom Fleming, by the way. And I'm sorry if I came across a bit weird back there, but…'

Realising a look would be better than all the explanations in the world, he shifted his grip on her hand, and with a brusque 'Come and see' dragged her towards the house, up the back steps and into the kitchen.

Three large packets of unopened mail lay on the floor, while the letters from a fourth were scattered across his kitchen table.

'This last package just arrived today,' he said, nodding at the one on the table.

'Fan mail?' she said, turning to look at him as if to check if she should know him. 'What are you—a TV star masquerading as a country vet? Or is this one of those reality programmes—life as it is for a country vet?'

She studied him intently for a moment, then shrugged. 'I suppose they wouldn't choose a downright homely vet for a TV series.'

'I am *not* in a TV series.' He cut off her speculation before she had a chance to get carried any further away. 'And it's hardly fan mail. But look at the amount of it, all from women who fancy they might want to marry me. And as well as that, though both Pat and the magazine were careful not to say where I live, at least eight women have sussed me out—tracked me down to Merriwee—and turned up on my doorstep.'

His visitor laughed.

'Which is why you hide out in the kennels?' she asked, clapping her hands in gleeful delight.

'There's nothing funny about it,' he told her. 'And I wasn't hiding—I'd just finished checking Rover's plaster and was coming out when you arrived.'

He paused then waved his hand towards the bulging packets of mail, adding grimly, 'What the hell am I supposed to do with all of this?'

'Answer it?'

She bent with a lithe grace—and a beguiling upward movement of the skimpy skirt—and lifted a letter from the floor as she hazarded this guess, then sniffed at it.

'Scented paper—I thought that went out in my grandmother's day. Where do they come from? What magazine? And who is Pat?'

Tom tore his eyes off his visitor's legs, sighed and sank down into one of three mismatched chairs that graced his kitchen table.

'Pat's my stepmother, and apparently the magazine in question ran a series of articles on lonely country bachelors who were all looking for a wife. One wife each, that is, not the one wife for all of them. Pat saw the articles and wrote to the magazine, to tell them they'd missed out on the most eligible of all. Namely me! I didn't see the letter, but she must have said something special because I can't believe all the poor blokes in the original story ended up with this many letters. The women write to the magazine who send on the letters to me via Pat but, as I said, a bit of good detective work has brought a number of them to my door.'

'And none you met were any good?' his visitor—Anna—asked. She was straightening the letters on the table into piles and the way she leaned forward, the way her hands moved, distracted him.

'It's not a matter of them being any good or not,' he growled, angry with himself for being distracted—by legs, by hands! 'I don't want a woman.'

It wasn't until she gave a little start he realised he'd

yelled the words at her, but the look she shot him was more assessing than shocked.

'Do you want a man?' she asked, her unfamiliar accent meaning he took a moment to process the question. A moment too long as she followed it up with a gentle, 'Is that difficult in a country town? Being openly gay?'

His head felt as if it would burst with irritation.

'No, it's not!' he stormed, then hesitated. 'Well, it might be in some towns—but it is in some cities, too, so it's not a "country" thing.'

Tom was about to continue when he realised he'd got off track.

'And I do *not* want a man.'

That didn't sound too good either, so he tried again.

'Well, not as a partner—not in the sense your tricky feminine mind zeroed in on. I don't want anyone, do you understand that? I want to live alone—I *like* living alone. Probably not for ever, but at least for now.'

'Licking your wounds? Did some woman do the wrong thing by you? Hurt you terribly?'

Green eyes, softened by sympathy, scanned his face, and he was about to pour out his aggravation over Grace's behaviour when he realised it *was* aggravation he felt about Grace's refusal to move to the country. He'd been annoyed that his plans had been disrupted, and angry she could do it to him, but there'd not been any sense of a deep emotional loss.

'Not that it's any of your business, but wound-licking is the last thing I'm doing,' he told the nosy—if attractive—female. 'But if you really want to know, after ten years of being the only male in a houseful of women—even the blasted animals were female—being alone is bliss.'

Anna looked up from tidying envelopes into stacks and smiled.

'You want me to mess these up again? Do you need the

disorder to convince yourself you really rule your male domain?' She waved a languid hand towards the bags on the floor, but managed to take in the unwashed dishes in the sink and the dust he knew was gathering on the refrigerator.

He had to laugh, and though the 'red alert' voice reminded him it was dangerous to be laughing with this beautiful woman, one glance at the serious rock on the ring finger of her left hand reminded him he was safe from her.

Safe enough to find out more.

'So, another South African doctor finds her way to Merriwee,' he said. 'I wouldn't have thought it would be the kind of place listed in your medical magazines as "highly recommended".'

She chuckled. 'We slot in under a thing called an "area of need" scheme. Our qualifications are checked, of course, and we're only allowed to practise for up to five years in particular areas, but we are accepted without having to do any exams before beginning practice. I've always wanted to see the outback, and on a map Merriwee was about the most outback place on offer. You know, there's a real problem in Australia, getting enough doctors interested in practising outside metropolitan areas, so even towns a couple of hundred kilometres from a big city might be classed as an area of need.'

Tom nodded gravely, as if this was news to him, although he'd grown up in the country not far from here and had been in Merriwee for a year, so knew the problem at first hand.

'And now you're here, is it "outback" enough for you?' he asked, wanting to keep her talking as the accent he'd found irritating and hard to follow at first had now taken on quite musical cadences.

She smiled at him.

More red alerts sounded in his brain!

'I really don't know yet, but the cat's decided. Could we see the cat now, do you think? Would you have a look at her?'

He'd been so busy listening to her voice, and the warnings in his head, and watching those slender fingers sort his mail into piles, he'd forgotten the cat.

'I guess so, but my surgery's still open. I don't suppose the cat will get much worse in the next hour.'

'Your surgery is *not* open,' the beautiful blonde argued. 'I went there first. It is locked, although the sign says you're open from four to six.'

'But I'm on the premises, aren't I? My receptionist's on maternity leave and her replacement doesn't start until Monday. Normally, someone would be there, but I don't always get patients brought in—at least not without an appointment. Most of my work is with cattle on the surrounding properties—so I can't just sit in the surgery building in case someone comes, neither can I leave it unlocked, because of drugs and instruments. Everyone knows if the place is shut to walk around the back, and if I'm not there to come up to the house.'

'This is very strange,' Anna said. 'Is such a casual approach an outback way or an Australian way?' She sighed, and smoothed some loose tendrils of hair back from her face. 'I have so much to learn and I told Philip I would only be away six months.'

'Philip?' Tom echoed, though he guessed who the man must be before his unusual visitor waggled her left hand at him.

Then, as if attracted by the flashing brilliance of the stone, she turned the back of her hand towards herself and stared at it, before smiling across at him.

'But that's your answer,' she said, radiant with joy at whatever good idea she'd come up with. 'You must write and tell these women you have found someone who's just right for you. Tell them you are engaged. It will be quite easy as all you need to do is multiple copies of a single letter. Typing in the addresses of all these women will be a big job, but maybe you could pay a secretarial person to do it for you. Or your replacement receptionist might be able to do it. Then all she would need to do is a mail merge on the computer and it will print out envelopes and do the rest.'

Tom stared at her. She was right, but it was such a simple solution, why hadn't *he* thought of it?

He knew he should say thank you, perhaps even praise the brilliance of it, but the words stuck in his throat, while his mind searched for objections.

And found one.

'But what of the women who come personally? Won't they want to see my fiancée? Meet the woman I've chosen?'

'I wouldn't think so,' his visitor said bluntly. 'Particularly not if you tell them quite rudely that you're fixed up. You certainly didn't have any difficulty being rude to me, so you shouldn't find it hard.'

Tom was still staring, but this time because he was startled, not by her conversation but by the placid delivery of it—as if his rudeness was of no account to her.

Which it probably wasn't, but he felt put out that she could judge him so offhandedly!

He was still searching for a rebuttal when she added, 'Anyway, if anyone did want to meet the winner of the "Marry Tom Fleming" jackpot, you could always introduce them to me.'

She waggled her hand at him again.

'I even have my own prop to add authenticity to the claim. A diamond as big as a cattle tick.'

He gave up on the search for a reply, smart or otherwise. Anna's suggestion—and the brilliant smile she'd flashed his way as she'd offered it—had left him speechless.

While her presence in his house—in his kitchen, where he spent most of his time—was making him...

Uneasy?

CHAPTER TWO

TOM had just decided he'd leave a 'back in thirty minutes' sign on the surgery door and go look at Anna's stupid cat, if only to get rid of her, when he heard the rumble of a heavy vehicle coming down the drive.

'A patient?' Anna queried, leaving the mail alone and walking to the back door to look out—for all the world as if this was her house and her business, not his.

But he followed her to look himself at the new arrival, not at the way his visitor's body moved, though he couldn't help noticing that as well.

A battered old truck had pulled in near the surgery, but it was the huge horse-float behind the truck that caught Tom's attention. From the noise within it, there was one agitated animal inside.

He slipped past his uninvited guest and strode across the dusty yard, thinking, as he and all the locals did a thousand times a day, that they must surely have rain soon.

'Trouble, mate?' he called to the elderly man climbing down from the truck.

'You the vet?' the man asked, by way of reply.

Tom nodded, thrusting out his hand and introducing himself.

Anna followed a discreet distance behind, thinking how different this greeting was to the suspicious way the vet had reacted to her arrival.

'I'm on my way to Mainyard, you know the place,' the older man, Jim Blair, was explaining. 'They've a great stallion there, and I've booked Felicity to be serviced by her, so needed to get her there before she dropped the foal she's carrying, but the darned fool mare decided she'd do it on the way—well, that's how it seems to me. Could you take a look?'

Anna knew enough about horses to know mares came into season soon after foaling, and at home, broodmares booked to expensive stallions usually foaled at the home of the stallion. This saved moving both mare and foal, especially when the foal might suffer injury on the journey.

But surely this dry, barren country wasn't the breeding ground of champion thoroughbreds.

The two men were now at the back of the horse-float, letting down the ramp. This caused a thunder of hooves on the floor of the trailer while a distressed whinny split the air.

'Oh, my!'

The words were simple enough but Tom Fleming's rich voice said it all. Whatever he was looking at was no ordinary animal.

Anna moved closer, in time to see the older man sidle into the horse-float, obviously putting himself at risk by entering an enclosed space with an agitated animal. But his presence, or perhaps his voice—Anna could hear him murmuring—soothed the horse.

'Can you secure her off hind leg in some way to stop her lashing out?' Tom asked, as Anna moved close enough to see the patient—a huge draught horse. 'I'll whip over to the surgery and clean up then we'll see if we can find out what's happening.'

He turned to Anna.

'Hang about—I'll need your help.'

It was an abrupt but unmistakable order, but she was too intrigued by what was happening to take exception to it. And now she was almost at the base of the ramp she could see the mare's contractions and the sheen of sweat darkening the hair on the animal's flanks. The poor thing was working hard, but nothing seemed to be happening.

Tom came back, trundling a wheelbarrow laden with

bales of hay which he split and spread over the ramp. He disappeared again, this time returning with the same barrow but full of vaguely familiar instruments and sterilising liquids—although all the equipment appeared to be extra large in size. There were also a couple of ropes which made Anna wonder about the difference between large-animal and human deliveries.

'Do you use those to pull the foal out?' she asked, pointing to them as Tom pulled on a plastic glove that reached up past his shoulder.

He glanced at the ropes.

'If necessary,' he said calmly, and Anna shuddered.

'What about anaesthetic?' Tom was now smoothing lubricating oil over the glove without, in Anna's mind, a thought for his patient's comfort.

'I'll explain later,' he promised, as the mare's owner lashed her mighty hoof to the side of the trailer.

'Wouldn't it be easier getting her out of the trailer first?' Anna asked him, still thinking of the horse's comfort.

'And put her where? I'd have trouble examining her if she's moving around a stall, and I haven't a crush big enough to hold her. And there's also the possibility that the foal is stuck in the birth canal. If that's the case, moving the mare any distance could injure one or both of them.' Tom explained this politely enough, but his next words were definitely commands.

'Now, come around behind me, and stay there, but be ready to push my shoulder when I ask.'

The label 'mad' floated again through Anna's mind, but Tom's brusquely repeated 'Now!' had her obeying. She moved cautiously up the ramp and stood behind him, watching as he lifted the mare's tail and thrust his hand and arm into the animal's vagina.

Did mares have vaginas or were they called by another name in horses?

She was wondering about this when she saw Tom

wince, and picked up the movement of skin and muscle that told her the mare was having another contraction. She could only imagine what pressure the strong squeezing motion must be putting on Tom's arm.

'Push now,' he grunted, as the rippling movements stopped, and for an instant Anna imagined he was talking to the mare.

But when he repeated it—'Now, woman! Push now!'— she realised the mare probably wouldn't have understood his order anyway, and she put her hand on Tom's shoulder and pushed.

'Harder,' he said, his voice husky with effort. 'Put your whole body into it—lean hard on me. I've got to work out how the foal is lying and I'm flat out reaching one foot.'

The words were distorted by the fact that his face was pressed against the mare's rump but clear enough for Anna to understand what he needed. She put her whole body weight into the push and held hard, even when the animal rewarded them with a great burst of foul air and a shower of liquid.

'OK, I've got one foot, but the second one is stuck behind the head. I'm going to try to release it without ropes. Rest a minute, Anna, then we'll have another go.'

Anna pictured the scene inside the mare's womb. She'd seen enough foals born to know they usually came into the world forefeet first, with their heads tucked between their legs, not unlike a person diving into water.

'OK!' Tom said, and Anna put her effort into helping him reach as far into the huge animal as possible. 'Stay there, nearly got it.'

Anna was soaking wet, gagging on the smell of urine, perspiring freely and panting with exertion, but she'd been caught up in the spirit of the job and was determined to do whatever she could to help the stricken animal.

'Ease up!'

She straightened, wriggling her shoulders to unkink

them, then stepped back to give Tom room to withdraw his arm.

'Now, let's see how she goes on her own,' he said, addressing the mare's owner, not Anna. 'If she's not too tired she should be able to finish her labour naturally.'

'And if she is too tired?' Anna asked.

'We'll do a Caesar,' Tom said casually, as if performing the operation on an animal this size was all in a day's work. 'That's one of the reasons I didn't want to anaesthetise her earlier. Too much anaesthetic altogether. We use epidurals on large animals just as you do on humans, but if I'd given her an epidural, she'd have lost the feeling in her legs and would have had to deliver lying down. Which would have meant me lying behind her on the ground and doing the same thing in a far more awkward position.'

Anna imagined the situation and was pleased she, too, hadn't had to lie on the ground.

But before she could agree with his assessment, he smiled and added, 'Gee, you look a mess!'

He grinned at her then turned back to watch his patient, and Anna, who should have been reminding him he was no oil painting himself right now, was so flustered by that cheeky flash of white teeth and the teasing humour in his voice, her mind went blank.

You can't be flustered by a smile, she told herself, then chuckled as she realised how right he was. She undoubtedly looked a mess. She'd lost her hat and long strands of hair had slipped free from the ponytail she'd combed it into before leaving the house, and they now clung damply to her face and neck. The odour from her clothes was intensifying in the still warm sunlight, and her damp shirt was smudged with suspicious traces of other byproducts of a horse's intestines.

But going home to clean up wasn't an option. She was part of this operation now and she was going to see it through. In fact, seeing a Caesar on an animal this size would be fascinating—though she hoped for the mare's sake it wouldn't be necessary.

She did, however, cross to a garden tap she'd spied earlier, over near the surgery, and splash water over her face and arms. Then, deciding she was already wet, she also splashed her clothes, hoping to at least reduce the powerful smell clinging to them.

'Hey, she's doing it!'

Tom had released the mare's tethered foot earlier, but had remained out of kicking distance of the lethal hooves. Now he moved closer, perhaps assuming the animal would be too intent on expelling her foal to lash out at him.

Anna hurried back, in time to see the tiny feet—well, tiny in relation to the mother—emerge, then the head, tangled in the birth sac but just where it should be.

Tom caught the shoulders of the foal, taking its weight so that, when fully delivered, it wouldn't go rolling down the ramp. When the mare paused in her pushing, he called to Anna.

'Can you give me a hand? Spread some of that hay at the side of the ramp. Then as soon as it's fully out, we'll lift it onto the hay and Jim can bring the mare down the ramp. She can expel the placenta on terra firma.'

Once again, Anna found herself obeying instructions, spreading hay then reaching out to help Tom catch the foal as the back legs were delivered. He had already ripped the birth sac away and the newborn animal snorted in its first breath of air, then lashed out with weak but still effective hind legs, catching Anna in the abdomen.

'Instinct,' Tom said, as Anna winced then shifted her grip so it couldn't happen again. 'Come on, we'll put it on the hay—though it's not an it, it's a little colt.'

'Not so little!' Anna panted, following him off the ramp then squatting down to thankfully release her burden. The colt looked around, then doubled his rickety legs under his

body and tried to stand—the efforts ma
with delight.

'Back off now,' Tom warned, using inst
his barrow to tie the already cut umbilical
comes Mum and she might be possessive.'

He was preparing an injection now, turning to A
he lifted it to check on air bubbles.

'Oxytocin—same stuff you use to help contract
uterus, only a slightly bigger dose for the horse. I'll injec
her with that, and an antibiotic when she's expelled the
placenta.'

Anna stood to one side of the ramp and watched the
way Tom's fingers moved as he prepared the second injection, fascinated by the similarities between human and
animal medicine.

Jim backed the big mare down the ramp, talking to her
all the time, rubbing his hand down her nose and telling
her what a wonderful girl she was.

'A colt, eh?' he said to Tom. 'That's great. The mare
carries bloodlines that go back to when my grandfather
started breeding heavy horses, so a colt will keep the male
line going.'

He spoke gruffly but Anna sensed the practical conversation covered a deep-felt emotion, and she was sure she
could see a suspicious wateriness in his eyes.

Not that she hadn't had to blink back a few tears herself.
Birth was a miracle which never ceased to affect her.

Then, as they watched, the wobbly legs straightened
and, miraculously, the little colt stood up for the very first
time.

Anna was so delighted she spun around to give the nearest person—who happened to be Tom—an exuberant hug,
then for good measure she kissed him smack on the lips.

Shock slammed through her, so sharp she felt a gasp of
what was almost pain. The vet looked no less shocked,
though he recovered more quickly than she did. Or perhaps

...rhaps his shock had been at

...m and said calmly, 'Want to ...ntil the foal's steady enough

...urned anxiously back towards

...bly do with a break after what

... You're welcome to stay at the ...dded quickly. 'Then, when you're ready to ...ove on, I've a big double horse-float—we could fashion a sling in the second stall so the foal's still close to his mother but not in danger of being kicked or trampled or falling and hurting himself.'

Jim nodded and made a gruff noise that could have been thanks, then, as the colt finally got all four legs working together, he hurried over to help support the wobbling animal and guide him towards his mother.

Tom's other visitor, meanwhile, was squatting on the dusty drive, watching the antics of the newborn foal with a smile of such delight it lit her entire face to a luminous kind of radiance. Somewhere in the operation Anna had lost her hat, and he could see the streaky fair hair, some still held back by a rubber band, though most had come loose and clung wetly to her smooth skin.

She'd obviously had a wash, because her wet T-shirt now clung to well-shaped breasts. But she was still a mess, he reminded himself.

And a woman.

And engaged!

Or was the engagement ring another ploy? Something to lull his suspicions while she wiled her way into his affections?

He looked at her again, and smiled wryly to himself. He was becoming as paranoid as she claimed her cat was.

Mess or not, she was utterly beautiful—the kind of woman who could attract any man she wanted. So wiling her way into the affections of a lowly country vet was about as likely as the foal he'd just delivered becoming a racehorse.

But, boy, did her kisses pack a punch...

'You got a stall or yard where we can put them?'

Jim's question reminded him of more important issues, and he turned his attention to them.

'No yard with grass on it, unfortunately. I was irrigating a couple of paddocks for a while, to keep some green pickings for patients, but my dam's about dry. I've got a big stall, and some grain and lucerne for feed. Give me a few minutes to spread some bedding straw in it, then we can settle them in.'

Tom strode away, glad of an excuse to get away from the distraction of the beautiful woman—a distraction that was nothing more than a physical reaction, exacerbated by his prolonged—but self-inflicted—celibacy.

'I'll give you a hand.' Her voice came from right behind his shoulder, and as she drew level he realised her stride easily matched his own.

'I've had horses—well, one horse,' she said, perhaps interpreting his sideways glance as doubt. 'I *do* know how to throw bedding straw around.'

She smiled, and as his celibacy-weakened body re-acted—mightily—to that smile, his head wondered how the hell the idiot called Philip had ever let her out of his sight—let alone agreed to being parted from her for six months!

They spread the straw, filled the water trough, checked the feed bin was clean, then stepped out of the stall as Jim, carrying the big foal, led the mare inside.

'There are small grain bins all along the wall of the tack room next door,' Tom told Jim. 'Help yourself to whatever you think she'll need.' He was about to turn away when he remembered the green feed. 'The lucerne's in the barn just beyond the tack room.'

'I'll get that for you if you like,' Anna said, ignoring Tom completely but smiling at Jim. 'How much do you need?'

'I thought you had a cat needing attention,' Tom growled, while Jim, perhaps conscious of the waves of disgruntlement Tom knew he must be giving off, assured Anna he could manage.

Not that she seemed in any hurry to move away. She was smart enough not to approach the foal too closely, but was obviously fascinated by its newborn wonderment as it tested its ability to stand and move and look about.

'The cat?' Tom reminded her again, and she turned towards him, a faint flush painting the fine, clear skin a delicate pink.

'I suppose we should get back to her,' she said reluctantly, then she smiled. 'But he's so beautiful, he's hard to leave, isn't he?'

Jim beamed at her, as proud as he would have been if the remark had been directed at him.

'He's that, all right!' he agreed. 'A real beaut! And you've been a real good sport, too, miss.'

She flushed again at the compliment, but as she finally tore herself away from the newborn colt to accompany Tom back towards the house, it was the word intriguing her.

'Beaut! That's an Australianism, isn't it?' she asked. 'And it means more than beautiful, doesn't it?'

Tom glanced at her and saw the tiny pucker of a frown, as if she was giving this matter as much concentration as she had given his problem with the letter-writers earlier.

'I suppose so,' he agreed. 'It means great, terrific, wonderful, but is used as a noun as well as an adjective.'

His visitor nodded, as if the explanation was acceptable.

'About the cat,' she said, switching the subject with such

rapidity that if he hadn't had two sisters he might have been startled. 'Now you've invited Jim to stay, you probably don't want to come over to the hospital.'

'Whyever not? He'll be busy with the horses for a while, and even when he's done he certainly won't expect me to entertain him. I'll tell him I'm going and that he can mosey on up to the house whenever he feels like it—take a shower, help himself to a beer or something to eat.'

The frown reappeared. 'But he's a stranger, isn't he? Yet you'd leave him in your house?'

Tom smiled as he realised what Anna was getting at.

'It's called country hospitality,' he explained. 'Because I've offered it, Jim won't abuse my trust. One day, I might be stuck somewhere and need a bed for the night. It's not often people are turned away out here in the bush.'

Anna stared at him for a moment, then shook her head, and Tom guessed that she neither understood nor fully believed him. And if the concept of trust threw her, boy, was she ever in for a steep learning curve about other aspects of country life!

Tom moved away, heading back towards the stall, but Anna was still worrying over this mad idea of Tom leaving a stranger on his own in his house. With a horse-float to load everything into, Jim could strip the place in no time. Not that there would be much to strip if the kitchen was anything to go by!

'And speaking of country hospitality—' Tom had materialised by her side '—I think both of us could do with a quick shower. I've even a selection of women's clothes so you should be able to find something clean to put on after it.'

Anna peered suspiciously at him.

'Don't tell me women send underwear as well as letters,' she said. 'My mother used to talk about girls throwing underwear at some pop star—back when she was growing up.'

He laughed again, and was still chuckling to himself as he said, 'That's a better assumption than the other one a woman might make—that previous women in my life had left the stuff. Actually, it's clothing my sisters keep here— presumably because it's past its fashion use-by date. But up here no one would care, so they can wear it around the place when they come for holidays.'

Anna wanted to ask more about these sisters, but he strode off, leaving her with no alternative but to follow. A shower and clean clothes—the offer was too good to refuse.

'There's a clean towel, soap, even shampoo, I imagine, in the bathroom right through there,' he told her, when she entered the kitchen to find him stripping off his wet and smelly shirt. 'I've a second shower out the back. I use it most of the time, so the girls leave their stuff in that bathroom.'

Anna heard the words, but her mind wasn't processing them. It was too busy taking in the sight of a tanned, sleek torso, so beautifully and precisely muscled it could have been a bronze cast of the perfect male body.

Well, not all the body—just the top half.

She saw his hands move to his waist, unbuckling his belt, and realised she'd better stop this open-mouthed— figuratively, not literally, she hoped—inspection of this stranger. If he wasn't used to having company he was likely to strip off right there in front of her.

So she should move...

'Through there,' he said, snapping undone the stud on his sturdy work trousers and indicating the door with a jerk of his head.

The words and movement broke the spell and Anna practically sprinted through the doorway, down a short passage and into the bathroom. Once there, she slumped onto the edge of the bath, her knees too weak to support her.

'You're going weak-kneed over a male torso?' she muttered to herself, then looked up, afraid she'd been overheard because Tom tapped on the door then poked his head and one arm around it.

'Plastic bag for your dirty clothes.' The hand at the end of the arm dropped a plastic supermarket bag onto the bathroom floor. 'The girls' bedroom is next on the right. The stuff's in the cupboard and drawers. Help yourself.'

His head disappeared and she heard his footsteps retreating, but when she stood up the weak-kneed phenomenon persisted.

'Nonsense!' she told herself, stripping off her clothes—with difficulty considering the state of her knees—and shoving them into the bag. 'He's just a man—and a practical one at that—and there's nothing special—apart from a terrific body—and a peanut-chocolate voice—about him...'

The shower was running hot by now so she stepped beneath the steaming stream and concentrated on ridding her hair and body of the stench of horse urine.

'Hurry up in there if you want me to see that cat!'

Once again he must have poked his head inside the bathroom door because she wouldn't have heard him so clearly otherwise. Apparently having sisters had led him to ignore bathroom privacy, she thought to herself as she turned off the water—pleased it had been hot enough to envelop the room in a dense fog—and rubbed herself at least partially dry.

She wrapped a capacious towel around her naked body, opened the door to check the passageway was clear, then made a dash for the room he'd indicated. Two single beds suggested it had been furnished with visitors in mind, and the fittings—a dressing-table with an old embroidered doily on it and a cupboard with a silk rose attached to the doorhandle—told her the usual visitors were female.

Anna opened a drawer and found underwear, but obviously for a much younger or smaller woman than her. Besides, the idea of wearing someone else's underwear wasn't all that appealing.

Yet again she was startled by a door opening and a hand appearing in the aperture. This time the hand dropped a plastic-wrapped package.

'Thought you mightn't like someone else's underwear, but the girls often pinch mine which seem, by some mysterious metamorphosis, to fit both of them. This pair's new.'

His footsteps told he'd retreated again before she properly made sense of what he'd said, but the package proved to be a new pair of hipster briefs in sensible denim-coloured cotton.

Gratefully, Anna ripped the plastic off and pulled them on, then tried another drawer and found a range of shorts—including a pair she was reasonably sure would fit. She was buttoning a big shirt she'd found in the cupboard when he knocked again, but this time didn't poke his head in.

'Ready?'

'One minute,' she called back, turning to the dressing-table and deciding using someone else's brush was better than walking around with wet tangles in her hair. Minimally!

Exactly one minute later Anna was out—her hair hanging wetly on her shoulders.

'OK, let's go see the cat!' He was waiting in the kitchen and took her by the elbow as if he'd known her all his life.

Was there such a thing as country familiarity?

Similar to country hospitality?

But the touch was nice—non-sexual and non-threatening. A friendly gesture, and one which warmed the lonely place inside her which she'd been trying to deny was there.

She'd think about the heat it generated later...

He took her down the shallow steps then guided her towards a battered, dust-covered vehicle that might once have been pale blue. She knew from the bulky shape it was one of the four-wheel-drives which were common on country roads, and she was wondering how he'd feel if she wrote 'Wash me' in the dust when a loud jangling noise made her shy away from Tom, turning back towards the surgery from where it had emanated.

'Is it the burglar alarm?'

She hoped it wasn't—she wouldn't have liked to have said 'I told you so' to Tom.

'No, it's the bloody phone. When I turn the sound up so I can hear it in the yards or stables, it changes character and makes that terrible racket. Excuse me a minute.'

He dashed towards the small building, hauling a bundle of keys from his pocket as he ran. Within moments he was out of sight—then the noise stopped.

But he was no less hurried coming out, jogging across the stretch of bare ground and once again grasping her arm.

'Never rains but it pours. Another pregnancy emergency, but this time it's your baby, Doc, not mine.'

'What do you mean, my baby?' Anna demanded, as he hustled her into the passenger side of the dusty four-by-four, then darted around the bonnet and climbed in beside her.

'Human.'

CHAPTER THREE

TOM started the engine, slipped the vehicle into gear and took off with a screech of rubber and skid of pebbles beneath his wheels. Neither did he slow down once on the bitumen roads beyond his grid. In fact, they roared through the town so quickly Anna looked around, certain a police car should be following them.

Tom was silent until they'd left the houses far behind, then turned off down a corrugated dirt road.

Anna clung to the handle above the door as they ricocheted across the top of the corrugations.

'There are different views on driving over these roads,' he told her, smiling at her obvious apprehension. 'Mine is if you go fast enough you don't go right into every rut. The patient's Dani, my receptionist. They've got fifty acres out here. Run goats. She's not due for another eight weeks, and her husband's away—he's a truckie.'

Anna made a mental note of 'truckie' for her Australian thesaurus, then concentrated on the real issue.

'But it won't be my job to deliver the baby. I haven't started work yet. Dr Drouin is in charge until Sunday.'

'He's up at the rodeo up at Placid Springs, and I heard only this morning that Peter Carter, the private GP in town who's officially on call, is in bed with summer flu.' Tom threw this explanation at her as he screeched to a halt in front of a gate.

He waited a second then snapped, 'Well, don't just sit there, get the gate!'

'Get the gate?' Anna repeated, puzzled by the order yet beginning to feel the anxiety Tom was obviously suffering.

'Open it!' he roared, and she all but fell out of the car in her haste to obey.

As she swung it wide and he drove through, she realised it made sense. If left to the driver, he'd have had to have got out, opened it, got back into the car to drive through, then got out again to close it.

She made another mental note—passengers opened the gates!

The wild ride eventually came to an end outside a small, low-set bungalow.

'Is she having contractions? Is that the problem? Eight weeks to go—thirty-two weeks—it's very early.'

'I don't think she's in labour, just really crook.' Tom was already out of the car, sprinting towards the house, but Anna still heard his reply.

Crook? Obviously not as in criminal, though a friend in Melbourne had used the word that way. Perhaps it meant ill.

She'd opened the door, dropped down to the ground, and was hurrying after him, pleased she'd had time to have a shower but wondering now what the patient would make of her in the baggy shorts and too-big shirt. Though this might be more appropriate attire for the country than her own clothes.

So much to learn...

At least her patient wouldn't know Anna was wearing Tom's underwear.

Following Tom into the house, she realised Dani wouldn't be worrying about anything—particularly not the doctor's attire. The woman slumped on the couch was seriously ill.

Tom knelt beside her and put his arms around her shoulders.

'What happened, Dani?' he asked gently.

'Feel sick,' Dani replied.

'We need to get you straight to hospital,' Anna told her,

kneeling in front of the woman and studying her flushed face and unfocused eyes. Anna pressed her fingers into the puffy, swollen ankles and saw the indentations left behind. The hypertension and oedema were obvious and no doubt a blood test would reveal an excess of protein in Dani's blood. The three symptoms of pre-eclampsia, a condition dangerous and potentially—should it move to eclampsia—deadly for both the pregnant woman and the child she carried.

Dani needed hospitalisation—but how? Wait for an ambulance? Even at the cracking pace favoured by her chauffeur, it seemed to Anna to have taken an age to drive here—and what if an ambulance wasn't available?

'We'll take her,' Tom said, as if he'd read her thoughts. 'I can lift her, you go ahead and open the car door.'

Anna didn't argue, though she did race through the small house to grab a pillow and a blanket off the double bed, carrying them with her and spreading the blanket on the back seat of Tom's vehicle, then pushing the pillow up against the far door.

'She should be lying down,' she explained, as Tom reached the car with his semi-conscious burden. 'I'll squat beside her so she doesn't roll off the seat.'

He didn't argue, simply leaning in and settling Dani down on the blanket, then frowning as Anna wedged herself into the space between the seats.

'Neither of you are restrained if I have an accident,' he pointed out, and Anna, who was tucking the edges of the blanket around her patient, glanced his way.

'Then don't have an accident!' she said, and turned her attention back to Dani.

Tom hurried around to the driver's side. Both the way Dani looked and Anna's reaction told him something was seriously wrong. Toxaemia of pregnancy? Animals could suffer the same thing. He took off carefully, then drove swiftly but cautiously back towards town. Behind him, he

could hear Anna murmuring to Dani, assuring her everything would be all right.

But would it?

Damn it all! He knew how much Dani and Brian wanted
this baby—how excited they'd been. This South African
doctor had better know what she was talking about!

And what she was doing!

Though she seemed caring enough, he'd give her that.

'Do you have a mobile? Can you call ahead to the hospital? Let them know we're coming in—tell them pre-
eclampsia. I'll need magnesium sulphate and whatever
anti-hypertensive drug they use.'

He slowed his speed slightly and reached out to activate
his hands-free, voice-activated mobile, speaking the number he knew by heart, not because he'd had reason to use
the hospital but because the sequence of digits was so close
to his own he often received misdialled calls.

'Emergency entrance will be best, they'll meet us there,'
Anna said, when he finally turned into the hospital entrance.

She was right. As he pulled into the covered bay, the
emergency doors slid open and a young nurse came out to
meet them.

Anna helped Tom lift Dani out and settle her onto the
gurney the nurse had wheeled into position beside the car,
then she helped push her patient into the small emergency
room.

'I've rung for help,' the nurse said. 'Dr Drouin's not
available, and Dr Carter, who's on call, is sick, but I called
Jessica—she's a senior—and she has midwifery experience.'

'Let's pray it's not needed,' Anna said, her eyes going
quickly to the nurse's ID where she read the name Elena.
'I'm Anna Talbot—I take over from Dr Drouin on
Monday. I don't think I met you when Elizabeth showed
me over the hospital.'

Elena introduced herself, and Anna, satisfied the nurse had accepted her as a person with authority, asked if the hospital had a file on Dani.

'I'll check,' Elena said, 'but I doubt it. She's probably Dr Carter's patient, and the records would be at his surgery. But neither of the doctors here do more than occasional checks on pregnant women, they don't do deliveries. Pregnant women go across to a bigger hospital on the coast to have their babies. They're usually under a specialist over there.'

'She intended going across to Rocky to have the baby,' Tom put in, using the locals name for Rockhampton, a regional city Anna vaguely knew was on the coast some hundreds of kilometres away.

'It would have helped to have a record of her normal blood pressure,' Anna said to Tom, as Elena disappeared. 'We diagnose pre-eclampsia with a systolic pressure of 140 or a rise of 30 mm over the patient's normal systolic reading, and 90 mm or a rise of 15 mm diastolic above her normal diastolic.'

She was taking Dani's blood pressure as she explained, and had to swallow a small gasp when she saw the mercury rise and rise. Elena returned with a file that proved to be an admission form, not a record, and she was followed by a youngish woman in paint-spattered shorts and a checked shirt.

'The shirt's clean,' she said, 'but Elena said it was an emergency, so I didn't stop to shower or change. You're Dr Talbot, aren't you?' she added, moving over to take Dani's hand, then addressing the patient before Anna had a chance to answer. 'And what have you been up to, idiot?'

Her voice was too softly affectionate for the question to be rude, and Dani responded with a wan smile.

'Feel awful, Jess,' she said, confirming Anna's guess that this was the midwife Elena had called.

'You look awful, too,' Jessica said heartlessly. 'Doesn't she, Tom?'

'Aw, I've seen her look worse,' he drawled. 'Remember when Bert Campion's sow stopped halfway through delivering her piglets and I was out on Westaway? She came home from that little adventure pretty sick-looking.'

'It was before we had the goats,' Dani protested. 'I'd only ever watched you do stuff like that! I had to go and throw up when I finished.' Though Dani's voice was weak, Anna realised Jessica and Tom had goaded the patient deliberately, bringing her back out of the black cloud her sudden illness had closed around her.

Anna checked the tray Elena had readied at Tom's phoned-in request, and was pleased to see the anti-hypertensive, which would reduce the dangerously high blood pressure, was one she knew and had used before. With that and magnesium sulphate, to ward off the possibility of seizures, injected into her, Dani and the baby she carried should be safe for a while.

'I'll need a urine sample,' she said to the two nurses when both drugs had been administered. Jessica stepped away from the bed.

'I'll do the catheter,' she said. 'Get a little of my own back on this woman who's had me doing unmentionable things to goats.'

Anna looked at Tom who was slouched by the top of the gurney, one of Dani's small hands enveloped in his capacious ones.

'Are you going to go out and give her some privacy?' she asked, and all three women laughed, though Dani's effort was weak.

'Tom worry about a woman's privacy?' Elena said. 'He's been in town long enough for us to get to know him and, believe me, he's more likely to poke his head under the sheet and have a good look. He's got about as much sensitivity as a block of wood.'

'Less, I'm sure,' Jessica said, returning from the basin where she'd scrubbed and dried her hands then pulled on disposable gloves. 'After all, blocks of wood probably care about their little splinters.'

Again the women laughed, and Anna shook her head in amazement at the casual camaraderie between them all. True, this was her first experience of working in a really small hospital, but surely they weren't all so informal.

She glanced up and saw Tom watching her, and felt a shiver of presentiment run down her spine.

He couldn't possibly know what she was thinking, and be watching for her reaction! Watching closely, as if her behaviour in this crisis was a test of some kind.

'Should we ring the fog?'

Elena's question, meaningless though it might be to Anna, snagged her attention away from tests *and* Tom's scrutiny.

'Ring the fog?' she repeated, when she realised it had been directed at her.

Jessica smiled.

'Flying obstetrician and gynaecologist—initials F.O.G. or FOG.'

'Oh, I remember reading about him. He's based south of here, isn't he? With a plane, so he can be anywhere in western Queensland within a couple of hours?'

'That's the man. He's purely a consultant, meaning a doctor has to refer the patient to him, but he does emergency work in any hospital in his area, which covers a large part of the state.'

Jessica explained all this as she busied herself with Dani's catheter, then she passed a small sample of urine to Anna.

'Test kits are in the scrub room just through that door over there,' she told Anna, indicating a closed door towards the back of the emergency room.

Anna took the sample, and Dani's chart, but she knew more was expected of her.

'I'll think about the FOG…' Her voice faltered over the acronym. 'But in the meantime, can you admit Dani and put her into a single room? I want someone with her all the time, with half-hourly obs. Do you have the nursing staff to handle specialling a patient?'

'They'll organise it somehow.' It was Tom, not one of the nurses, who delivered this statement, and though Anna assumed he had no authority at all within the hospital, he was so definite about it she took the assurance as gospel.

She walked into the small room Jessica had indicated. Once there, she remembered Elizabeth showing it to her on the tour and pointing out the cupboard where various test kits were kept.

'What's wrong? Is this pre-eclampsia you're talking about some kind of toxaemia?'

Tom's voice startled Anna so much she almost dropped the small box she'd pulled from the cupboard, but he'd appeared and disappeared so often since she'd met him, she shouldn't have been surprised to find he'd followed her into the room.

'Yes. And you can probably guess it precedes a far more dangerous condition—eclampsia. Pre-eclampsia can usually be managed with the drugs I've given her, one to reduce the blood pressure and the other to prevent seizures, together with complete bed rest. The condition causes various metabolic imbalances and subsequent kidney problems, but the symptoms disappear after the baby is born and the condition rights itself.'

She continued working as she explained, checking the test strip to confirm an excess of protein in Dani's urine. She frowned at the result, although she'd guessed what it would be.

'The problem is, any single one of the signs—oedema,

proteinuria or a rise in blood pressure—can lead to a diagnosis of pre-eclampsia, but Dani has all three.'

She was speaking her thoughts aloud—nothing more—and though Tom didn't say anything, she felt his presence made it easier to think through the problem.

'We can watch her closely. If her blood pressure rises again within the next six hours, then it's time to do something.'

'Like what?'

'Either induce the baby or take it by Caesarean section before she moves into the more dangerous eclampsia. As I said, once the child's delivered, the symptoms go away.'

She looked at Tom, and saw concern in his blue eyes.

'I'll ring this FOG person if Dani wants me to, or if the nurses think it's advisable,' she said, hoping to reassure him. 'Tell him the position we're in and see what he says.'

Tom nodded but didn't leave the room—well, not until he'd frowned at her for what seemed like ages but in reality had probably only been seconds. And when he did leave, he again poked his head back around the door, but whatever he intended to say remained unsaid as he merely shook his head, then disappeared once more.

Following Dani as she was wheeled from the emergency room to a ward—he wondered idly if single-bed rooms *were* called wards—Tom's mind was on the new doctor, while his shoulders were tight with a tension he hadn't felt since he'd arrived in Merriwee. He might have whinged about the letters, but they hadn't really upset him, and he'd been thrown by the arrival of the women who'd tracked him down, but he'd got over that.

No, this was something new.

Something different.

Something that had started back inside the little room. He'd gone in to ask about Dani's condition, then had intended thanking Anna for her kindness to his friend, but the words had stuck in his throat, blocked by the weirdest feeling of *déjà vu*—only *déjà vu* was the sensation of having been there before, while this feeling was more a presentiment of the future, a sense that the two of them...

What?

He shook his head in frustration.

He had no idea!

And he wasn't a fanciful man—in fact, he was about the most down-to-earth bloke he knew.

Maybe he was going mad.

Or sickening for the flu that seemed to be doing the rounds.

Tom closed his eyes then opened them again. The two nurses were shifting Dani from the gurney to a bed.

'You rest now, you hear?' he said sternly to her, then, to give himself something practical to do, he wheeled the gurney back to the emergency room and let himself out the door.

Satisfied with the test, Anna wrote a note on Dani's chart, then made her way to the nurses' station where she learned Dani was now in Room Six—three doors down the corridor.

The young woman was sleeping and Jessica, who'd been sitting beside her, stood up and moved quietly towards the door.

'I'm off duty but I'll stay with her overnight. We've been friends since we started school,' she explained to Anna.

Anna nodded.

'I'll be over at the doctor's residence if you need me, and if you don't call, I'll come back in an hour to see how she is.' She hesitated. Nursing staff in country hospitals at home often had to make life-or-death decisions without the benefit of a doctor being present and she guessed it was the same here. Jessica would have practical experience in these situations a newcomer like herself might never gain. *Would* never gain, given she only had six months.

She moved closer to Jessica, so she could speak without waking Dani.

'What do *you* think about calling in the specialist?'

Jessica didn't hesitate.

'Not yet,' she said firmly. 'He'll have to fly in and once he arrives, well…'

Now the hesitation *and* a frown, before she continued, 'Well, he'd be here on the spot and, rather than just take a look at Dani and fly out again, he might decide to take the baby—either by induction or a Caesar—just in case. Then, because it's premi, it and Dani will have to be flown to a maternity unit on the coast, which, with Brian away, Dani would hate. But if we can control this stage of things, the little one will have a better chance of remaining right where it is until it's far safer for it to emerge into the world.'

She stood up and moved away from the bed, steering Anna towards the door.

'A lot of GPs won't do deliveries these days, because of the cost of insurance. Insurance companies fear something may go wrong and they'll have to pay out liability claims later, so insurance costs have sky-rocketed, and local GPs just can't pay for obstetric cover.'

Anna nodded. 'I've heard all of this, but what's your point?'

Jessica studied her for a moment, brown eyes searching Anna's face.

'Would you be happy to deliver the baby if it became necessary? Would you feel confident doing a Caesar if Dani's condition suddenly worsened and she needed it done urgently—before the FOG could arrive?'

'Of course!' Anna replied without hesitation because she knew Jessica, anxious about her friend's safety, needed this reassurance. 'As well as the big obstetrics component in my medical training, I've done an obstetrics short course, and performed, I suppose, a hundred Caesarean operations. I believe the private doctor in town is willing to do anaesthetic work, so between us we should manage.'

She'd just finished this positive and, she hoped, comforting explanation when she realised she wasn't—yet— officially on the staff at Merriwee Hospital. But she wouldn't bother Jessica with that minor consideration.

'Yes, Peter Carter often helps out with minor ops,' Jess said, then she gave a satisfied nod. 'So that's settled, and as long as we have that back-up position in case things turn bad, I'd say don't call the FOG.'

Anna walked away but a sense of responsibility rested heavily on her shoulders and in the end she made her way to the main hospital office where she studied the list of phone numbers Elizabeth had shown her during the 'tour'. The office clock reminded her it was getting late, but she should at least let the official on-call doctor know what was happening—as a back-up position, as Jessica had said.

Just in case...

The woman who answered the phone sounded harassed, but her abrupt 'Jackie Carter speaking' told Anna she'd reached the right place.

Quickly she explained the situation, adding, 'I became involved because I was at the vet's place when Dani rang Tom to say she felt ill. Tom knew Paul Drouin was away, and your husband was sick so he took me along, but as Dr Carter is officially on call, I thought I should let him know.'

'Do you absolutely need him there?' Jackie asked, and Anna hastened to assure her that Dani was now resting comfortably and would be monitored all night.

'Well, Peter's asleep right now, and he's been so restless and fidgety all day I'd hate to wake him just to tell him all of this, but if you do need to talk to him, ring me again.'

'Some back-up!' Anna muttered to herself, then she

shook her head. In another two days this would be 'her' hospital, and there'd be no back-up then. This was the challenge she'd wanted—and in the place she'd heard and read so much about—the vast Australian outback.

She walked back to Room Six to check on Dani, and was relieved by Jessica's report that the patient's blood pressure had already dropped back to within normal range.

'Phone me if you have the slightest concern,' Anna told Jessica, 'and I'll come right back. If I don't hear from you, I'll check her again in an hour or so.'

The nurse nodded as Anna repeated this promise, then returned to sit beside her friend.

With only a couple of wrong turns in the hospital corridors—building the place around an open central courtyard made navigation complicated—Anna finally reached the rear staff entrance and crossed the parched earth towards her little cottage.

A light was on in her living room, but she was too tired to wonder why she'd had one on when she'd left the place in broad daylight. She dug in the pocket of her shorts for the key and, finding nothing, remembered the shorts belonged to someone else. And her clothes were in a plastic bag at Tom Fleming's place.

She'd left all the windows open, and though they were all screened against insects, maybe she could remove one of the screens and climb in. She moved to the closest window and was about to test this theory when she realised that not only was a light on in her house but the place was occupied. Tom Fleming was lying full length on her living-room floor, and after an initial shock—wondering if he had broken into her house then died in there—she noticed movement. And realised what he was doing!

He was talking softly to the cat, which was nuzzling lovingly around his head, then, as Anna watched, the wretched animal leapt lightly up onto his chest, curled her tail around her legs and sat there, for all the world as if she'd never had a moment's doubt about life in Merriwee.

Anger flared in Anna's chest. The chcek of the man, walking into *her* house, lying on *her* floor and seducing *her* cat with sweet talk!

She marched back to the front door and pushed it open.

'Well, make yourself at home, why don't you!' she snapped. 'Is privacy non-existent in the outback? Do people wander in and out of each other's houses at will? And what do you think you're doing with my cat?'

Tom lifted the cat from his chest and sat up, his large hands still cradling the animal.

'Curing her?'

The cat now had the cheek to curl herself up on his lap.

'I found your dirty clothes in the car and when the plastic bag jangled, I realised your wallet and keys were in your skirt pocket. So it seemed a perfect opportunity to check out the cat, which is why you'd come to me in the first place. And then, as I was coming this way anyway, I thought why not pick up a Chinese meal, as I'm starving and you're sure to be hungry and I really do appreciate all the help you've given me today—first with the foal, but especially with Dani. She's a good friend as well as an employee.'

He finished this speech and smiled, as if proud of the thought processes that had led him to break into her house.

Though if he'd used her key, maybe it hadn't been, technically, breaking in.

And now he'd mentioned food, she realised she was hungry...

'Well, I suppose that's all right,' she grouched, then stepped backwards as he removed the cat from his lap and stood up, his long, lean body so close she felt a sense of...not quite invasion and not quite apprehension, but too tingly a reaction for an engaged woman to be comfortable about experiencing. It reminded her of the heat she'd felt when he'd first touched her hours earlier, and just thinking about it brought a return bout, so heat and tingles mixed and mingled in a truly shocking manner.

To cover this physical chaos, Anna bent to pat the cat, but Cass, fickle creature that she was, ignored Anna's coaxing hand and continued showing devotion to the man, winding around between his legs as he walked towards the kitchen.

'You sit down while I bung the containers in the microwave,' he said, still ordering Anna around. 'I had no idea what you might like so I got a variety of dishes. I'll give you a hoy when they're all hot and you can come and choose whatever you fancy.'

Anna had another new word to consider. Did 'hoy' mean a call? She was puzzling over this when Tom re-emerged from the kitchen.

'You're not sitting,' he scolded, and ushered her towards the lounge, before pressing a glass of what looked suspiciously like white wine into her hand. 'Please, don't tell me you don't drink. Having a drink is almost obligatory in the outback. This is a very light white, and won't do you any harm, and we can drink to the birth of the colt.'

Realising it was futile to protest against this man's bulldozing behaviour, Anna sank down onto the seat and lifted her hand to accept the glass of wine.

The warm air had condensed against the glass and the beads of moisture caused her fingers to slip, but Tom's reaction was instant, seizing both her hand and, within it, the glass, and holding both steady.

Far from steady was the reaction of her heart, which, though the man had touched her many times already this afternoon—he was obviously a tactile kind of person— now suddenly found something intimate in this latest clasp of strong, slightly calloused fingers.

You're tired and hungry, Anna excused her strange internal behaviour, detaching her hand, now steady on the glass, from his and setting the glass down—just in case it wasn't hunger causing her palpitations and another touch might make her tremble.

Tremble? Her mind repeated the word in utter disbelief. Fortunately Tom had returned to the kitchen so she could carry on this internal debate without any fear of him picking up the vibes of her panic in the air around her.

'OK, food's up!' he called, though how much later Anna wasn't sure. She'd been sipping at her wine and trying to make sense of all the outlandish and unexpected things that had happened since she'd left her new home however many hours earlier to walk to town.

She stood up and cautiously undertook the journey into the kitchen, hoping it wouldn't become a similar odyssey.

'I had expected the outback to be different,' she admitted to the man who stood there, proudly displaying so many containers of food there'd be leftovers for a month, 'but I'm not sure how I'll cope if it keeps being as different as it's been this afternoon and evening.'

Tom laughed—Uncle Fred's laugh again—then said, 'You probably won't have to help deliver a draught horse every day.'

'Well, that's a relief!' Anna told him, and, though she'd have liked to have joined in his laughter, a small warning voice in her head suggested she was better off concentrating on serving herself some food.

Which, of course, would fix the palpitations she'd experienced earlier…

Tom watched Anna devour the food she'd heaped on her plate. A slender woman with a good appetite! The way she tackled it, she must have been starving, so it was good he'd brought food—good, too, he'd sorted out her cat. Two pluses to this visit, although he knew he hadn't come here for either reason. He'd come because he'd had to come.

Because, as he'd driven home from the hospital, he hadn't been able to stop thinking about her, and in the end any excuse would have done.

He *must* be mad…

CHAPTER FOUR

ANNA woke late the next morning with a sense of panic, as if she shouldn't have been sleeping late, then she remembered it was Saturday—two full days to go before she officially started work. On her final visit to the hospital to check on Dani—at two in the morning—she'd met up with Paul Drouin, back from the rodeo and tired but willing to take over responsibility for the new patient.

He'd assured Anna she'd made all the right decisions and, seeing Dani resting comfortably, Anna had known he had been telling the truth. So she'd gone home to bed and slept deeply, waking only when the sun rose high enough to shine directly through the window onto her face.

'Curtains. I'll have to get curtains or I'll never have a proper sleep-in,' she said aloud, though aware that talking to herself—the cat was nowhere in sight—could become a bad habit.

Climbing out of bed, she saw the clothes she'd discarded when she'd fallen into it. Clothes belonging to Tom Fleming's sisters—*and* Tom himself if you considered the underwear. She'd wash them and return them today—that way all connection to the man would be finished, and the strange sensations she'd experienced in his presence yesterday could be shut away in some far recess of her mind for ever.

Buoyed by this thought, though uncertain of the protocol regarding returning used underwear, she pulled on her robe, gathered up the clothes and headed for the kitchen where a tub and small washing machine had been installed in a cupboard.

The cat was back in her travelling cage!

'Oh, blast you, Cassie!' Anna said, then she decided maybe the cat just liked sitting there and would come out when she felt like it.

'You'd better!' Anna warned the animal. 'Because I'm not getting that man around to coax you out again.' She scowled as the cat shrugged its elegant shoulders and turned away, as if it was totally immaterial to her what Anna did. 'Haven't you ever heard of female solidarity?' Anna muttered at it, then went in search of her own dirty clothes.

They were in the living room, still tied in the plastic bag Tom had offered her, and she took them through to the little laundry alcove, dumping them in the tub and rinsing them under running water before shifting them to the machine. Then she set the lot to wash while she made herself a cup of tea and organised an easy breakfast of cereal and fruit.

But as she moved around the kitchen, uneasiness hovered like a ghost behind her shoulders. At first she blamed the cat, sitting in the box but swivelling her head to follow Anna's movements, but in the end she had to admit it was the memory of Tom Fleming—so at home in her kitchen the previous night—which was haunting her.

'Nonsense!' she muttered, spooning cereal into her mouth as if food might, again, provide an answer to her problem.

But the uneasiness remained, leaving her only when she retreated to the living room where his spectral presence was less noticeable.

Two hours later, with the washing she'd hung in the tropical sun already dry, she determined to get rid of all reminders of her strange afternoon and evening. She folded the borrowed clothes—though not the underwear, she'd buy a new pair the same colour and size and give him those—into a basket, scowled again at the cat, which remained stubborn and aloof in the open cage, and headed across to the hospital. She'd visit Dani then drive over to the vet's, and once she'd dropped off the clothing she'd explore some of the district around the town. Someone had told her of a dam not far away, where people fished and swam and even sailed small skiffs.

She'd have a look at it, and then go the museum, and generally learn her way around Merriwee.

The plan went well until Anna pulled up in front of the vet's surgery. Once again the place looked deserted, but this time no dusty vehicle suggested its owner was somewhere on the premises. Even Jim's truck and horse trailer were missing. Had he moved on?

With or without Tom's furniture?

Anna crossed to the stall where they'd settled the mare yesterday and saw her there, her son suckling lustily.

'So your friend Jim won't be far away,' she said, reaching up to rub the big mare's nose.

She stayed for a few minutes, watching the colt move on legs that still splayed endearingly, then headed back towards the house, nervous and uncertain now she was approaching it.

Stop being fanciful, Anna told herself. It's just as well there's no one here. You can leave the clothes on the veranda without getting involved in conversation or rescue missions. Just dump them on a chair and go—or perhaps they might be safer on the kitchen table. After all, Tom had made himself at home at her place, so he could hardly object to her taking two steps into his kitchen...

Anna crossed the yard and took the low steps in a single stride. The front door was open and, thinking there could be someone inside, she knocked and called out, but was greeted by silence. An unlocked house was still a novelty—in fact, it was closer to a shock—so, no matter how much she justified it to herself, she still felt very much an intruder as she walked around the veranda towards the kitchen.

It was as deserted as the rest of the place, though a half-empty cup of tea or coffee, resting on a pile of magazines on the kitchen table, suggested Tom might have been called away suddenly.

Anna looked around—the letters were gone from the table, and the packets he'd said held more mail had also disappeared. Maybe she'd imagined that part of the most unusual afternoon she'd spent with Tom yesterday.

She was so intent on her thoughts that a loud jangling noise made her jump. As it continued, she looked desperately around for its source, finally realising it was the phone and remembering Tom's explanation about the modified ringing tone.

'You'd probably hear it over at the hospital!' Anna muttered to herself, pressing her hands to her ears to stop the terrible demand. Not that it helped much—the noise seemed to penetrate flesh and bone and was now clanging in her brain. Stopping it became a matter of self-preservation, and without much further thought, Anna reached out towards the wall-mounted instrument and lifted the receiver.

'Vet's place!' she said crisply, hoping that answering someone else's phone wasn't a serious offence in Australia.

'Who's that?' a young female voice demanded.

'Anna Talbot, I'm the new doctor at the hospital. I came over to see the vet…' To return his clothes? Not good, Anna! '…about my cat, but there's no one here. Answering phones that ring is kind of automatic with me.'

Silence greeted this—to Anna—quite logical explanation.

'Where's Tom?' Suspicion made the words sharp, but to Anna there also seemed an edge of desperation in them.

'I don't know, but he's not here. As I said, I came—'

'About your cat, yes, I know, but I need to talk to Tom or at least get a message to him.'

'I could get a message to him,' Anna volunteered. 'I'm right here at his house. I can leave a note on his kitchen table then, if it's urgent, I can keep phoning the house to make sure he gets it as soon as he comes back.'

'I don't know!' There was a sob in the girl's voice now, and a pause so long Anna wondered if they'd been disconnected.

'Who did you say you are?'

Anna explained again, then added, 'Maybe if you tell me the problem, we can sort something out between us.'

Another long silence, then, 'Look, this will sound stupid, but I'm Tom's sister, Patience. There are two of us, me and Penny. It's Penny I'm phoning about. You see, she was unhappy at school and Mum's not long ago remarried and she really, really, really wanted to see Tom—Penny that is, not Mum—so I've just put her on the plane to Three Gorges.'

Another stifled sob at the other end then the explanation continued.

'I couldn't tell him until she was on the flight or he might have told Mum or tried to talk Pen out of it, but now she's on the plane and it lands at Three Gorges at two, and it's an hour's drive from Merriwee, but you probably know that, but if we don't get on to Tom soon then Pen will be stranded at the airport in Three Gorges. I didn't think about him not being at home. Penny's only thirteen!'

Anna understood the panic on the part of the sister back in Brisbane, where flights to Three Gorges originated. But her heart went out to the young girl on the plane, already unhappy, coming in search of a beloved brother only to find he wasn't there to meet her.

'Look,' Anna promised, 'I'll stay here and wait for your brother, and if he isn't back in time to drive down to Three Gorges and meet the plane, I'll go myself.'

This offer was greeted by relief, but so quickly followed by doubt that it took some time for Anna to work out a plan whereby a series of phone calls would ensure Penelope's safety, just in case she, Anna, might turn out to be a kidnapper.

An hour and a half later, Anna stood in the lounge at Three Gorge's airport and watched the passengers disembarking. It wasn't difficult to work out which one was Penelope Fleming as she was the only unaccompanied child. Though she didn't get off the plane for so long after the rest of the passengers Anna was beginning to wonder if the phone call had been a hoax. As she came closer, Anna saw the young girl was exactly as her sister had described her. The blunt-cut fringe and straight fall of black hair on either side of the young face framed wide-open eyes so dark a blue they were almost navy.

The dark hair and blue eyes must be the father's heritage, Anna decided, as no one seeing Penelope and knowing Tom could doubt their relationship.

'Hi, I'm Anna,' she said, approaching the girl and holding out her hand. 'I was at Tom's house when Patience phoned to say you were coming, and I told her if Tom wasn't back in time to come down and collect you, I'd come myself.'

The blue eyes studied her for a moment, then darted around the small lounge, scanning it, no doubt, for her brother.

Was it because she couldn't see him that she sidled closer to Anna?

'You spoke to Patience?'

'I did,' Anna confirmed, as the girl continued to study the occupants of the lounge while almost hiding behind Anna. 'She rang from the airport as soon as your plane took off but, because I'm a stranger, Patience suggested you call her on her mobile and confirm this, then I thought you might like to phone Merriwee hospital—I'm the new doctor there—and ask for someone who's met me to tell you what I look like so you know it's really me.'

'And not some kidnapper!' the child said, a grin lighting up her rather sombre face. She sighed then stepped back a little, as if the possibility of being kidnapped was somehow reassuring.

Two phone calls and half an hour later, they were on the road.

'The nurse at the hospital said you were South African, and you do have a funny accent so I guess that's what it is,' Penny—as she'd asked Anna to call her—said. 'She described you well, too—the tall blonde part anyway. She didn't know the colour of your eyes. They're green, aren't they?'

Anna, aware of the huge road trains that thundered down these outback roads, was concentrating on her driving, but agreed her eyes were green.

'This is awfully kind of you.' Penny was obviously the kind of child who felt obliged to make conversation. 'It was a bit of an emergency, getting up here to see Tom. We're telling Mum it was because…'

And so the story came out—first a brief family history that made Anna's heart ache when she considered the significant losses Tom had suffered in his life. Then the tale of a man successfully disentangled from one—in the sister's eyes rapacious—female, and now the target of who knew how many more desperate women.

'The problem is, he's hopeless at saying no to women, because he was brought up to be polite and thinks saying no is rude,' Penny explained, causing Anna to conceal a smile. It must be sisterly love blinding the child to his true character, as the man had had no trouble at all being rude to herself the previous afternoon. She mentioned this, but Penny saw it as another symptom of his confusion.

'See, he must be stressed by the letters. Tom's never

rude! And if he's stressed, he'll pick the wrong one for sure.' Penny's tone indicated just how dire this result would be. 'That's how he ended up engaged to Grace,' she continued. 'And, would you believe, Ghastly Grace was actually on the plane. That's why I had to get off last and kind of hide behind you until she'd fixed up a hire car at the counter and actually left the terminal.'

Apart from the liberal sprinkling of 'actuallys' in the conversation, the explanation was quite succinct, though Anna couldn't help but wonder how the man she'd met the previous afternoon was going to take his sister's arrival.

Or a thirteen-year-old interfering in his life!

'And what did you say you were doing at his house?' Penny asked, and Anna smiled to herself. Was the child adding her to the list of women to be beaten away from her brother?

'I've got this cat,' she began, then decided Penny didn't need to know all the details, so she explained about Cassie, letting Penny think that had been the reason for this morning's visit.

'No one was there, but nothing was locked—well, the surgery was, but the house was wide open.'

'No one locks up in the country—it's one of the things Tom likes about it,' Penny explained, but it soon became obvious she hadn't been diverted by this side issue. 'And did you say you knew Tom?'

This time Anna let the smile escape.

'No, I didn't say, but I only met him yesterday—about the cat—so I'd hardly say I know him. And although he must be an absolute chick magnet for you and your sister to be so concerned over him, he's safe from me, Penny. Look!'

She waggled her left hand in Penny's direction.

'I've got a man of my own waiting for me back home.'

Penny demanded details of this man—details which

Anna found surprisingly hard to provide. Words like kind, considerate, busy—'he runs a big international company'—wouldn't convey much to a teenager. Neither did Penny seem to understand why someone who was engaged to be married would voluntarily part from their fiancé for six months.

Well, she wasn't alone in that, Anna remembered as she continued answering Penny's questions. Philip's family, Anna's own parents and most of her friends had been vociferous in condemning her folly. Even Philip, though he said differently, failed to fully understand her need for this period of freedom before settling down to be what everyone expected her to be—the perfect corporate wife!

Trying to explain—'I think it was because I've always done what other people wanted or expected me to do that this six months doing something different and adventurous for myself was so important'—as much to reinforce her reasons in her own head as to enlighten Penny, kept the conversation rolling until they reached Merriwee and bumped over the grid and down the dirt road leading to the vet's place.

'Gosh, look at the line up of cars. I've never seen the big truck and horse-float, but the dusty four-wheel-drive is Tom's, and I guess one of the other two is the car Grace hired. But he must have someone else visiting as well.' Penny beamed at Anna. 'At least with three lots of visitors he won't be able to get really angry at me, will he?'

The trusting faith of a thirteen-year-old, Anna thought, but she did agree to accompany the child into the house just in case big brother wasn't as welcoming as he might be. Carrying Penny's suitcase, Anna once again ascended Tom Fleming's front steps, but this time she followed Penny around the veranda, pulling up short behind the girl who was lurking just out of sight of anyone in the kitchen.

But close enough to hear the conversation.

'Will you get this through your admittedly attractive

heads?' The not-so-chocolaty voice reverberated through the air. 'I definitely do not want an article written about my pitiful bachelor state, or photos taken, or an in-depth look at why women responded in droves to my berserk stepmother's letter. And, Grace, you made your choice a year ago when you broke off our engagement, so what you think you'll achieve by arriving here like the cavalry on a charge, I don't know. Now, I have work to do, a house guest to feed, patients to see and a new colt to check out, so will you both, *please*, leave.'

Penny pressed back against the wall, but neither woman appeared.

'We should go in, not eavesdrop,' Anna whispered, as a cajoling woman's voice begged the man to listen for just a moment.

'No, wait,' Penny whispered back, as the second woman started to explain that she was going to do a story on him anyway, so he might as well co-operate.

At this stage, the first woman—presumably Grace—began to argue with the second, pointing out that as Tom was still more or less engaged to her, there *was* no story.

'I can't believe this,' the male voice said, the words so despairing Anna acted without thought for the consequences.

'Come on,' she muttered to Penny, grasping her by the arm so she could drag her into the kitchen if necessary. 'We'd better break this up before they start tearing each other to pieces.'

Penny came willingly enough so they breezed into the kitchen together, though Anna's heart was thudding and her knees so shaky it was a wonder they weren't making castanet noises. She hated any kind of confrontation, and this one looked as if it could get nasty, but she couldn't walk away.

Summoning up her brightest smile, she bestowed it on

the man she'd come to rescue and her voice, when she finally made it work, sounded calm enough.

'Look, Tom, I've a wonderful surprise for you. Patience rang after you left to say Penny was on the plane so I whipped down to meet her.'

Tom stared in total bemusement at the pair of them, then he caught Penny in his arms as she hurled herself at him. Shock kept him silent while Grace and the reporter woman—Anna thought she had said her name was Carrie—both demanded to know the identity of the new visitor.

'Oh, allow me to introduce you,' he said, remembering in a flash of sheer, overwhelming brilliance Anna's solution to his mail problem. 'This is Anna, my fiancée.'

He set Penny aside, and reached for the tall blonde beauty, raising her left hand in the air.

'See!' he said. 'All done properly, right down to the ring. So, Miss Reporter, you're too late for your story on the outback's last eligible bachelor and, Grace, I'm sorry you've wasted your journey but, as you see, there's nothing here for you.'

He hitched his arm through Anna's then, seeing Penny's scowl, drew her close as well.

'Just play along!' he whispered at Pen, feeling mutiny humming in her rigid body. 'I'll explain later.'

Anna looked stunned, Grace looked as if she might explode, while the reporter did explode, but only into speech, not literally.

'Is she one of the women who wrote after we printed the letter? How did you choose her? Did she send a photo? Did you go on looks alone? What's your name?' This was addressed to Anna, who was still looking so taken aback Tom had to hide a smile. 'Where are you from, Anna? How long have you known Tom?'

He held his breath, but his visitor rallied and soon proved she was equal to the task.

'I think you'll have to excuse us,' she said, her accent making the words seem more an order than a request. 'Penny's had a long and tiring trip and she hasn't been well, which is why her mother sent her up here, so Tom and I need to see her settled.'

Anna took Tom's arm, ignored the tremors touching him caused—though she and Penny had gorged on chocolate on the drive so she couldn't blame hunger—and steered them out of the kitchen.

'What do you mean, claiming me as your fiancée?' she demanded in a fierce whisper as soon as she felt they were out of earshot.

'You suggested it yourself,' Tom shot back at her. 'Yesterday. You offered!'

His rebuttal was all but drowned out by Penny's accusing words, delivered in a tone of stern recrimination to Anna. 'You told me you didn't know him—that you'd only met him yesterday! You told me a lie.'

Oh, boy! Anna thought. What a mess, and where, given this man is already causing problems in your hitherto stable and reliable body, do you go from here?

But she set aside her own problems to concentrate on Penny. Truth was important to young people, and the girl had already had an emotionally fraught day.

'I didn't lie to you, Penny, but let's wait until we're sure Grace and the other woman have left before I explain.'

She then rounded on Tom, who was the cause of both her internal and now these new external hassles.

'But I think you have more explaining to do than I have. My suggestion was simply that you tell the women who wrote to you that you'd found someone, not that you claim me as a fiancée in front of your ex-fiancée and a reporter.'

She glared at him, mainly because he didn't seem in the least bit chastened by her scolding. In fact, if she'd known him better, she might be able to tell if the twinkle in his eyes was a trick of the light or a gleam of extremely ill-timed amusement.

Before she had time to give further consideration to the suspicious twinkle, the unearthly clangour of the phone startled them all, and Tom disappeared to answer it.

Leaving Anna alone with Penny, who'd stomped over to the window and was staring out of it.

'They're leaving now, though, if I know Grace, she'll be back,' the young girl announced, just as two car doors slammed in quick succession and the sound of engines starting eased a little of Anna's tension.

She crossed the room to stand beside the teenager.

'I'm not engaged to Tom,' she said quietly. 'He just used that as a way to get rid of the two women. When I met him yesterday he was telling me about the letters, and women tracking him down to Merriwee and visiting him in person. I suggested he tell them all he'd already found someone. OK, so that was a lie but it was a kind way of putting them off without hurting their feelings. I guess he remembered that idea when we walked into the kitchen and those two were hassling him.'

Penny turned and her face lit up as she smiled.

'Really?'

'Really!' Anna confirmed, and knew they were friends again when Penny gave her a quick hug.

'I don't know what you're looking cheerful about, kid!' Tom's voice broke them apart. 'I haven't even begun to consider your behaviour, Penny Fleming, but when I do, you mightn't smile again for a month. Right now, I have to go out on a call, and as I don't want to leave you here on your own on your first afternoon, you'd better get out of that skimpy dress and into some sensible gear and come with me.'

The growled invitation must have reminded Penny she might still need support, for she turned immediately to her new friend and said, 'You told me you don't have to start work until Monday. Why don't you come, too? It's fun, going out on Tom's calls. You get to see all kinds of interesting stuff.'

Tom looked as if he'd just as soon take a venomous snake along for the ride, but Penny was squeezing Anna's fingers and Anna guessed she wasn't quite ready for the confrontation with her brother.

'OK,' she agreed, 'but if your brother can wait another couple of minutes, you should also phone your mother. Just to let her know you're safely here with Tom.'

'And that you didn't kidnap me,' Penny added, grinning at Anna.

'What was that kidnapping stuff all about?' Tom demanded, as Penny skipped away. 'And while we're on the subject of Penny, would you mind telling me just how you happened to know Penny was arriving? Is this some plan you've been involved with from the start? Was yesterday's visit, over a cat you claimed was paranoid yet seemed perfectly fine to me, just a ploy to check out the ground before dumping Penny on me?'

No twinkle in his eyes now, and just enough recrimination in his voice to rile Anna.

'You're the paranoid one.' She jabbed her finger in his direction. 'Seeing conspiracies where none exist. As for dumping Penny on you, all I did was rescue the child from the airport then rescue *you* from a tight spot with your arguing women. And for this I'm getting accusations.'

The accented voice bit the words off sharply, but Tom barely heard, mesmerised instead by the indignation sparking in the green eyes and the faint flush which anger had swept into her cheeks. And this time he knew it wasn't celibacy causing the gut-clenching uneasiness inside him, but the sure knowledge that he was attracted to another man's woman.

The red alerts should have warned him—should have ensured he did everything in his power to avoid this woman for however long she stayed in Merriwee. But had he listened?

No!

He'd blamed his libido and now he'd entangled the two of them for at least as long as Grace and the reporter woman remained in town.

'Well, don't you have anything to say for yourself?'

Her aggravated demand shook him out of his state of shock, and he looked vaguely around, wondering what she'd been saying when the lightning bolt of desire had struck him senseless.

'She was saying you should be thanking her, not getting cross with her,' Penny told him, returning to the room with the remote of the phone clutched in one hand. 'And Mum wants to talk to you. She says you're to put me on the next flight home, where she'll deal with me—but you won't, will you?'

The plaintive plea was accompanied by a pleading look, and Tom, who'd missed his sisters more than he'd realised possible, gave in.

'Hello, Pat. The brat's safe and sound, and as far as I'm concerned it's OK for her to stay until the holidays, if it's all right with you. I'll see Maureen up at the school and ask if they'll slot her into a class there so she's not getting away with this behaviour scot-free.'

He heard Penny's groan and frowned at her, daring her to argue with this plan, then cut short Pat's apologies for the girls' behaviour, explaining he had to go out on a call.

'What's the call?' Penny demanded, as soon as he'd disconnected. 'Something gruesome like the time the wild steer had torn its leg on barbed wire and you had to tranquillise him then stitch it up?'

Tom forgot he was angry with her and grinned.

'Nothing so exciting. We're going out to Bob Filmer's stables. He's got a young filly he wants branded and blood-typed and a hair sample taken for DNA for the stud record books.'

'Branding—I don't think I want to watch that,' his other visitor said, so quickly Tom guessed she'd been searching for an opportunity to escape the outing.

Or his company?

That thought niggled him but, really, he could hardly blame her. The poor woman had been thrust into the Fleming family problems—though she'd coped admirably with the engagement announcement and he'd be eternally grateful to her for rescuing Penny from the airport. But wasn't it better if she didn't come with them?

Wasn't it better for him to see less of her, rather than more?

Of course, while all these thoughts were flashing through his head, Penny had taken over again, forestalling any attempt on Anna's part to escape the outing.

'Oh, branding's OK now,' she was saying. 'Tom heats the brand with liquid nitrogen, like doctors use to burn lumpy bits of people's skins. Then he just presses it on. It hardly hurts the horse at all.'

Tom watched as Anna responded to this explanation with a laugh that lit her face to a luminous beauty. His guts knotted even tighter.

Definitely should see less of her...

'I've had one of those lumpy things—usually keratoses caused by sun damage—burnt off the back of my hand,' she said, but she slung her arm around Penny's shoulders as if she meant to accompany them. 'And while it might not hurt at the time, the wound can be sore afterwards, so have some pity for the little filly.'

'Not me!' Penny argued. 'I'm going to be a vet like Tom, and Tom says vets can't be ruled by maudlin pity or try to put human feelings onto animals.'

The green eyes slanted his way, as if the woman was

reassessing him. But if she made something of Penny's remark, he couldn't tell. Her face was as inscrutable as an oriental mask.

A very beautiful oriental mask.

CHAPTER FIVE

ANNA accompanied the pair out to the car, though she knew she should be making some excuse and escaping the immediate vicinity of the good-looking vet. But if she did that, she'd be letting Penny down, and she couldn't bring herself to face the hurt in those huge blue eyes.

Perhaps if she concentrated on the technical aspects of the call, she'd be sufficiently distracted to not notice Tom as a man.

And she'd sit in the back seat, so she could avoid looking at his strong, well-muscled body.

'No, you sit in the front,' Penny insisted, foiling the first of Anna's plans.

She concentrated on the other.

'This call—to brand a horse, take blood and hair—doesn't seem urgent. Why do it on a Saturday afternoon?'

She glanced Tom's way but managed to stay focussed on his left ear—a relatively safe choice seeing she'd never found ears particularly sexy!

But she didn't turn away quickly enough to miss the sideways look he flicked in her direction, his blue eyes smiling in such a bone-melting manner she was glad she was sitting down.

'Bob's the local chemist and a good friend. He works during the week and opens the shop on Saturday mornings as well. He does get up at some ungodly hour every morning to train his horses before he goes to work, so I suppose I could have done it then, but Saturday afternoon is the best time for him, and I wasn't doing anything else, so why not do it now?'

It was the kind of question to which there was no answer, but Anna found the silence uncomfortable and silently blessed Penny when she broke it.

'Before DNA, how did they keep records of horses?'

'With what they call a passport, Pen,' Tom answered, swinging the car across the railway line then turning in a direction that was new to Anna. 'Racehorses in particular still have them, but with the DNA included. The passport has things like markings, hair whorls—'

'Hair whorls?' Anna queried, caught up now in the discussion for its own sake.

'Like a human's cow-lick,' Tom explained. 'Horses tend to have at least one somewhere on their body, though clever tricksters could use a razor to manufacture one if necessary.'

'Manufacture a cow-lick?' Penny's disbelief reverberated through the car. 'Whatever for?'

Anna wondered as well and waited for a reply, forgetting that she didn't want to look at the man and studying his strong, straight profile and the way his eyebrows twitched slightly as he considered his answer.

'Say you have a horse with no markings—no white socks or nose blaze—and it's trained to race but isn't very fast. Then you find another horse that looks just the same, but races well. You go to the races, and your first horse, which is no good, gets really good odds from the bookies—fifty or a hundred to one. But you've done a swap and brought the better horse to race in its place. You back it and rake in the money.'

'But that's cheating!' Penny protested, and Tom laughed.

'Not only cheating but against the law, and more than one horse trainer has ended up in jail for doing it.'

'But can you stop that kind of thing happening, even with the horse's DNA registered somewhere?' Anna was interested in spite of herself. 'I imagine horse DNA tests take as long to run as human ones, so the stewards at a racecourse can't be doing it prior to a race. And once the race is over, and the punters have their money, no one could take it back from them.'

They turned into a stable complex as she finished speaking, and Tom pulled up in a clean-looking yard.

'It's illegal to profit from crime, so if the fraud's discovered later, and the perpetrators caught and proved guilty, any money they made from the hoax can be recouped.'

He'd turned towards Anna to explain, but though the words were practical enough—no way could words like 'hoax' and 'recouped' be considered even vaguely flirtatious—they started a quivery kind of chain reaction in Anna's skin cells, so she shivered in the warm afternoon air.

Bad move when the man involved was so tactile. He immediately reached out to touch her arm.

'Are you all right? You can't possibly be cold. I know I've had the air-conditioning on but it's not making much of an inroad on the temperature, given it's about forty degrees Celsius today.'

The blue eyes raked across her, as if some physical symptom might reveal the cause of her shiver.

Anna wanted to tell him she was fine—just fine—but the concern in his eyes diverted her momentarily and before she found even the easiest of answers, Penny interrupted.

'Aren't you coming?'

She'd disembarked immediately they'd stopped and was now pounding on the driver's side window.

'Bloody child!' Tom muttered, touching Anna lightly on the back of her hand before turning to respond to his sister.

He climbed out of the car, ignored Penny, urging him towards the stables, and came around to open the passenger door. He might be temporarily muddled by his extreme reaction to the new doctor—and no one would blame him, given she was an utterly beautiful woman—but that was no excuse to forget his manners.

Anna slid to the ground, her long, golden-tanned legs gleaming in the late afternoon sunlight, and images of those legs wrapped around his body swam in Tom's head. A cool, slim-fingered hand touched his.

'My turn to ask if you're all right,' she said, her voice lowered so it sounded like unfamiliar music in his ears.

'Of course I'm not all right,' he grumbled, pulling himself together sufficiently to make the words sound brusque. 'But it's not something a doctor could cure, so you can put away the black bag.'

He caught a glimpse of hurt in the green eyes before she swung away and strode towards the stables, where Penny waited in a patch of shade. Following more slowly, he thought about the peculiarities of attraction. He had four bags of mail from women wanting to meet him, and hadn't felt interested enough in meeting *any* woman to bother opening more than ten or twelve of the letters. Then a blonde-haired beauty had swanned into his life, messing with his practical, sensible mind—hurt green eyes, yet— and reminding his body of its sexual needs.

Bob must have heard their arrival, and by the time Tom reached the stables he'd come out and introduced himself, then, practically drooling over Anna, had led the two females inside. Tom cursed himself for dawdling. He should have realised how a woman-chaser like Bob would react to Anna.

By the time Tom entered the cool shady building, grumbling only slightly to himself, Bob was already making a pass.

'I'd be delighted to have you ride any of these horses,' he said—oh, so smooth! It certainly wasn't Penny being favoured with this offer.

'Want to try your hand at track work?' Bob continued. 'Riding them on the track as part of their training?'

Anna asked, running her hand down over the velvety muzzle of Bob's race-winning gelding. 'I don't know that I'm good enough for that.'

'Nonsense! I'd show you what to do,' Bob assured her, reaching out to pat the horse himself. Some excuse! It was obvious all he wanted to do was touch Anna's hand.

'Let's go!' Tom said, determined to interrupt the flirtation before it went any further. He'd have liked to have pointed out the engagement ring to Bob, but it was a bit hard to bring it casually into the conversation.

'Right!' his friend replied. 'You got your gear?'

Looking down at his hand when Tom knew full well it wasn't carrying his bag was a stupid act, but he did it anyway, then muttered all the way back to the car to fetch the damn thing.

He returned to find Penny and Anna in the small yard beyond the building, cooing and carrying on over the newly broken-in filly—which was, he had to admit, a little beauty.

'She's bred for distance and one day she'll win the cup,' Bob said.

'The cup? They have a Merriwee Cup race?'

Bob laughed at Anna's question—far too heartily!

'Well, they do, but I'm talking about the Melbourne Cup—biggest horse race in Australia. It'll be on in a couple of months. The whole country stops for it.'

'For a horse race,' agreed Anna, rolling her eyes.

'It's not just *a* horse race,' Penny explained. 'It's the cup!'

Anna looked comically baffled by this sporting enthusiasm—a look she did delightfully, of course—and when Bob started to explain again, Tom decided he'd had enough and turned the conversation firmly back to business and the task of branding the young filly.

'I don't think I'll watch,' Anna said. 'Is it OK if I go back to the stables?'

Bob assured her it was and looked as if he was about to escort her there, so Tom reminded him he'd have to hold the filly still.

'I'd have asked Anna to help,' he added, seeing a small window of opportunity, 'but she'd probably put the poor horse's eye out with the rock she wears on her left hand.'

Bob flashed a look towards the stables, then turned back to Tom.

'Engaged, is she? Well, that should make things doubly interesting!'

'She's engaged to Tom!' Penny announced, and the look on Bob's face told Tom they were both equally flabbergasted, though Bob managed to put it into words.

'She is? Wow! Sorry, mate, I didn't realise. Are you ever a dark horse, going on about being off women and enjoying a bachelor existence, when all along you've got a beauty like that stashed on the sidelines!'

Tom opened his mouth to explain that was only a ruse, then closed it again, deciding he wouldn't mention it. Though Penny knew it wasn't true, so why had she said it?

'He was all over Anna like a rash,' Penny explained a little later, while Tom was using liquid nitrogen on the brand and Bob had made an excuse to go across to the stables. 'And I could see it made her uncomfortable. I thought if he thought she belonged to you, he'd back off.'

'People don't "belong" to each other, Pen,' Tom said carefully, hoping his internal reaction to Anna 'belonging' to him hadn't been obvious on the outside.

'Actually, I think they do,' Penny argued. 'I don't remember our father, but Patience said he and Mum belonged together, and now I see Mum with Keith I understand because there's a kind of belonging thing happening there as well. It's as if some people are just meant to be together, actually, like bread and butter, or fish and chips!'

'I can't wait to tell Pat you think her relationship with

Keith is like fish and chips!' Tom said, chuckling at the idea and ruffling his sister's hair. 'But maybe you've got something. During all those years after Dad died, Pat met a lot of men, and none of them clicked until Keith came along. But I think that's a different kind of belonging, Pen. It's a sharing kind of belonging. There's no element of ownership in it.'

Penny looked puzzled, which didn't surprise Tom. He felt a little that way himself because he had no idea where the thoughts he'd just put into words for his sister had come from. It wasn't as if he'd ever spent a lot of time thinking about relationships. In *his* life, they just seemed to happen.

Usually disastrously!

However, the conversation didn't faze Penny for long. With a cheerful, 'I'll go and chase him away from her,' she departed for the stables, leaving Tom alone with the filly.

'Stallions don't have half the trouble human males have,' he told the beautiful animal. 'Though I don't doubt you'll cause some excitement on the racetrack when you're older.'

All three humans reappeared while the filly was still considering her reply, Anna explaining she'd been roped in to assist in the branding.

So Bob would get a chance to jostle against her—Tom's thoughts were growing positively poisonous!

He calmed himself enough to do what had to be done, and though Bob did try a few obvious—at least to Tom— manoeuvres, Anna avoided contact so skilfully Tom realised she'd probably been putting up with infantile stuff like that most of her life.

'Thanks for your help,' he said, when they'd said goodbye to Bob and were walking back to the car. 'Thanks to both of you.'

'It was fun,' Penny assured him. Then she turned back

as if to check she wasn't going to be overheard. 'But if you go over there to ride his horse, I'd watch that Bob, Anna. Even though I told him you were engaged to Tom, he was still trying to flirt with you.'

Anna stopped dead and turned to the young girl. 'You told him I'm engaged to Tom? But you know I'm not, Penny. I explained that. It was just a ruse to get Tom out of a tricky situation.'

Penny grinned at her.

'I know that—it's why I thought of using it again when he was coming on to you so strongly.'

Anna shook her head. It was OK for a couple of women just visiting the town to think she was engaged to the vet, but for locals to hear this story?

'Don't worry about it.'

Tom must have sensed her dismay, for he touched her lightly on the shoulder then, with his hand still resting warmly against her shirt, guided her towards the passenger side of the car.

'Even if Bob mentions it to anyone, it will be a nine-day wonder then die a natural death.'

He smiled, the laughter in his eyes reminding her of Penny's cheeky grin.

'And if it doesn't, we could stage a spectacular "break-ing off the engagement" scene in the middle of the main street. You could even fling that monstrous engagement ring at me if you liked.'

Anna closed the fingers of her right hand around the ring. Talking of it, feeling its sharp edges, reminded her of Philip—and that she shouldn't be feeling the things she was feeling in the presence of another man.

'I don't think so,' she said quietly, silently praying he was right about the nine-day wonder and hoping that's all it was for her as well as the locals.

'Anna's real fiancé has his own jet,' Penny announced as they drove back towards town.

Anna saw Tom glance sideways at her, as if querying this statement, but she was too busy trying to remember how she could possibly have talked so much on the trip between Three Gorges and Merriwee that she'd mentioned Philip's plane.

'He has offices all around the world,' she said, feeling a need to defend what some might see as extravagance on Philip's part. 'It's easier to get around to all of them with a private jet, rather than relying on commercial flights. Getting the right connection with commercial flights can often mean overnighting somewhere you don't need to be and cause a day or two's delay.'

Again a glance, but this one openly sceptical.

'And would that be disastrous? Would stock markets crash? The world oil price sky-rocket? Gold shares plummet? Is he so important, your Philip?'

Anna decided to ignore both the supercilious questions and the snide way in which they had been asked. It was none of Tom Fleming's business what Philip did, and if Penny hadn't been in the car with them, Anna would have told him so in such a way it would have left no room for error.

She folded her arms and turned pointedly away from him, looking out the window at dry ploughed fields awaiting rain for planting. But Penny answered for her, surprising Anna again at the amount of information the child had wheedled out of her on the trip to Merriwee.

Tom absorbed the information, telling himself it was only natural a woman as beautiful as the one who sat in stony silence beside him in the car would attract the attention of a rich and powerful man.

'It's because of Philip she's a doctor.' Penny finished her recital on a note of triumph, but what he'd heard already had soured Tom's stomach and he certainly wasn't going to ask either of the females to explain this remark.

What he was going to do was avoid all further contact

with the older of the two—and possibly strangle the younger if she insisted on telling him more details he didn't want to hear.

Avoiding Dr Talbot was easier thought than done, Tom realised when he bumped into Anna for the fourth time in the next three days, though on this occasion—they were standing together in the queue at the supermarket—they had enough time to do more than exchange polite hellos.

Enough time for him to register her clothes as well. Had she sewn two skirts together that this one reached almost to her knees? And the cheeky daisy thongs were gone, replaced by sedate sandals.

Though there was a tiny flower adorning the bright red nail polish on her big toe. She wasn't going to conform *too* much to country standards!

'I suppose we could make a "we should stop meeting like this" joke,' she said, drawing his attention back to her face. Big mistake, as her flashing smile made his heart gallop around in his chest while her light-hearted tone told him she was over the snit his asking about Philip had caused.

He was trying to think of some extraordinarily witty reply when she suddenly leaned back against him.

'Enemy women at ten o'clock!' she murmured, and looked with rapt devotion into his eyes. He glanced in the direction she'd indicated and saw Grace and Carrie—he'd confirmed that was the reporter's name when the intrusive woman had arrived on his doorstep at eight on Sunday morning—zeroing in on them.

The bright glare of flashbulbs temporarily blinded him, and caused a flurry of excitement among the checkout girls.

'Damn,' the woman who was disentangling herself from his arms muttered crossly. 'I should have learnt by now that getting involved in doing a favour for you—no matter how small—always leads to complications.'

She slid behind him and muttered her curses into his back, adding, with a fair amount of pique, 'Couldn't you have shopped earlier in the day?'

He was about to remind her that it had been *she* who'd leaned against *him*, making the photo possible, when the customer in front of him moved on, and it was his turn to unload his groceries onto the counter.

'We heard you were engaged, Tom,' the checkout girl, Barbara, was cooing at him as he shuffled into place across from her. 'Is your fiancée someone famous that you're having your photo taken?'

Tom quickly considered, and equally quickly discarded various replies—such as *She's not my fiancée, but apparently* her *fiancé is famous*—eventually settling on a bland, 'Oh, haven't you met Anna? She's the new medical superintendent at the hospital.'

'You're a doctor?' If he'd said she was an astronaut Barb wouldn't have sounded more surprised. She studied Anna, still cowering cravenly behind him, before pronouncing solemnly, 'You look more like a model or an actress.'

By this time Grace and Carrie were waiting at the end of the narrow aisle where he and Anna would eventually exit, both wearing the identical looks of women who were not about to be denied whatever it was they were after.

His skin, most probably!

Barbara was cheerfully shuffling his groceries past the scanner so escape was impossible, though Anna hadn't given up hope of avoiding a confrontation.

'I think I might turn around and put my groceries back on the shelves,' she whispered. Her earlier animosity was obviously forgotten as she sought an ally in this awkward situation.

'Don't you dare,' he told her, then, to ensure she didn't

escape, he told Barb to add the cost of Anna's groceries to his total.

'I'll pay for the lot,' he said expansively, with a mental 'so there' to the absent Philip.

But eventually they had to leave, and then put up with Grace and Carrie falling into step with them, one on either side, like some bizarre kind of guard frog-marching them out of the shopping centre.

'We know who Anna is,' Grace announced.

'*And* that she only arrived in town on Thursday,' Carrie added, a note of triumph in her voice.

'So how can you possibly be engaged?' This from Grace who was on Tom's side, so close her shoulder was brushing against his body on one side, while on the other he could feel Anna's angry rigidity as she marched stoically forward.

'Haven't you heard of the internet?' she snapped at Grace. 'Internet meeting rooms, internet dating, internet sex. I would have thought an up-to-date woman like yourself would know all about the latest technological advances in the mating game.'

'Internet sex!' Carrie barely breathed the words, but Tom's heart quailed as he thought of the spin an imaginative reporter could put on that! It was all right for Dr Talbot, she was only visiting this country and, anyway, she was beautiful enough to bluff her way through anything, but he'd have to leave town if such an article came out—and change his name before he resettled somewhere else.

'My car's this way,' Anna said, stepping away from Carrie's crowding and walking towards it, then realising Tom was carrying all the groceries, including cat food and the steak she intended cooking for her own dinner.

'I'll drop your groceries off at your place,' Tom said, as if his mind was tuned to hers. Then, to Anna's relief, he steered the other two women towards his vehicle.

It wasn't until Anna was belting her seat belt across her body that she admitted to herself the relief was more to do with escaping Tom's presence than getting away from the two women who were dogging his footsteps. When she'd gone in to visit Dani the previous morning, the first person she'd seen had been Tom—leaving the hospital after he, too, had paid a visit to his sick friend, although the official visiting time at the hospital wouldn't start for another three hours.

Then, when she'd pulled into the service station to refuel her car yesterday evening, he'd been pulling out, and again this morning, when she'd done a familiarisation round with Paul Drouin, Tom had been sitting by Dani's bed, for all the world as if he and not the absent truckie was her husband.

OK, so he was a caring and considerate friend, but did he *have* to visit so often?

It wouldn't have been so bad if her body didn't react every time she set eyes on him. She'd never been an overly sensitive person—not in a sexual or sensual way. Yet now it seemed as if her skin had been flayed by the outback dust, exposing nerve endings that leapt and tweaked and tingled whenever the handsome vet appeared.

With a sigh that made her windscreen mist over, she started the car and headed back towards the hospital, determined in some way to inoculate herself against the man's potent attraction.

Arriving home to a phone call from Philip helped, but unfortunately she'd no sooner hung up than Tom appeared, clutching her groceries and announcing with great pride that he thought he'd finally got rid of the two women.

'I promised Carrie that if she held off publishing a story now, we'd give her an exclusive for the wedding. Grace huffed and puffed about me making it all up, so I said of course it was on the level and we'd already fixed a date—the first of January. That OK with you?'

Anna stared at him.

'But we're not getting married,' she reminded him.

He grinned and dumped her bags of groceries on the table.

'I know that, and you know that, but Carrie doesn't, and the date made even Grace back off. I'd like to think it means we've seen the last of them, but Bob Filmer arrived at the supermarket as I was about to leave and, of course, seeing me with two women, zeroed in on me. Now Carrie's going to use him for the "last eligible bachelor" article and Grace seems to think if Carrie's staying she should as well. Or maybe she liked Bob's style of flirting.'

Anna shuddered, remembering Bob's over-the-top compliments and ogling looks.

'Good luck to her,' she said, then realised that, far from avoiding any opportunity to be with Tom Fleming, she was actually feeling both relieved by, and relaxed in, his company. Not good!

'Thanks for delivering the groceries, but I guess you'd better be off. You wouldn't want to leave Penny on her own for too long. Heaven knows what she might decide to do.'

'Oh, that's OK,' Tom said calmly, opening Anna's refrigerator and peering inside, then producing the half-finished bottle of wine he'd brought and opened on Friday evening. 'Jim's taking care of her. He stayed out of the way when the women were around, but once he came out of hiding I introduced him to Penny and the pair took to each other like long-lost siblings. Bit of an age gap, of course! Penny's busy trying out names on the colt, then the pair of them are going to the café for dinner to celebrate its birth.'

He waved the bottle of wine towards Anna.

'Would you like a glass? I'm on my way to visit Dani but I could stay and share one with you. A kind of celebratory drink that we've sorted out our problems.'

'"Sorted out our problems"?' Anna repeated but she nodded yes to the drink. After all, what harm could come of sharing one drink? 'When you've offered a magazine exclusive rights to a wedding that isn't going to happen?'

'But that's the beauty of it,' Tom told her, passing her a glass of wine, though this time she managed to avoid tangling her fingers with his. 'Because there won't be a wedding, we can't be liable for breach of contract or any other legal issue if the magazine decided to get nasty.'

'Legal issue? Breach of contract?' Anna took a desperate sip of her drink. 'Tom, you didn't sign anything, did you?'

He laughed and reached over to touch her reassuringly on the shoulder—tactile man in action again.

'Of course not, you silly duffer. I'm not totally stupid.'

Anna was reasonably sure that being called a 'silly duffer' wasn't complimentary, but the touch, and a warmth in his so-special voice, made it seem that way.

So much for inoculation!

CHAPTER SIX

TRUE to his word, Tom stayed only for a drink and, though the little house felt empty when he'd gone, Anna told herself it was only because he and Penny were the closest things to friends she'd made—so far—in Merriwee.

Though Penny doesn't make your skin tingle, she reminded herself.

Putting aside the matter of tingling skin—though it vaguely worried her that Philip's presence had never induced any physical manifestations in her skin—and looking at the situation sensibly, now that Tom's tale of a wedding would get rid of both his problem women, there was no reason why she need ever see him again.

'Even if it means me remaining friendless, and you sitting there for ever!' she told the cat who'd plunged her into this maelstrom, and, now that Tom had departed, had returned to sitting in her travelling cage.

Anna fed the cat, who deigned to cross the kitchen to eat, then cooked her own meal and carried it to the dining table, where she'd left a stack of patient files. Then, as she ate, she went through first the files, some dating back twenty years, of patients who were currently in hospital, then those of patients she would see at the surgery the following day.

Paul had explained the split in her duties, and how some patients would always see her as outpatients at the hospital, while others would come privately to the two sessions a day she held at Peter Carter's surgery.

'And if I'm called over to the hospital for an emergency during one of these private sessions?' she'd asked, trying

93

to work out when she'd have time in this schedule to breathe, let alone shop or eat or sleep.

'The patients wait, or Peter picks up the slack, or sometimes, if whatever it is isn't urgent and your call to the hospital might take time, the patient makes another appointment and goes home.'

'It all seems very slapdash,' Anna muttered to herself as she checked the file of a diabetic patient who, according to the notes, found it impossible to stick to his diet.

She set aside thoughts of her schedule and concentrated on ways she might be able to persuade the man to behave sensibly, for his own sake and that of his family.

As luck would have it, he was the patient who was with her when her first summons back to the hospital interrupted her session the next day. Fortunately she'd finished her examination and a stern lecture on the importance of his diet before the call came in.

'I'm sorry, it's a serious car accident. I'll have to go,' she told the man, Albert Hibbert. 'But make another appointment for next week, and take this chart and write down everything you eat—even snacks—and drink. We'll soon sort out where you're going wrong.'

Albert beamed at her.

'Ned said you were very pretty—he was right,' he said shyly, leaving Anna, as she hurried across from the surgery to the hospital, to wonder who Ned was.

'Single car accident, ran off the road and into a tree, two women injured but not as seriously as the ambos had first thought.'

Elena, once again manning the A and E entrance, passed on this information as Anna came in. 'Bruising and lacerations and one has severe swelling of the ankle. I've sent for Jillian.'

Jillian? Jillian? Anna sorted through the maze of information she'd been trying to absorb over a very short period.

'Nurse trained as an X-ray tech?'

Elena nodded.

'We've two —her and Roberta—and they do X-rays on a roster system except on Wednesdays, when the radiographer comes up from Three Gorges.'

By this time they'd reached the bed of the first accident victim and Anna recognised, with a spurt of sympathy and a splash of horror, that it was Carrie, the reporter. Almost fearing to look, she glanced sideways and confirmed that, yes, the second injured woman, now being wheeled towards the X-ray room, was Grace.

'What have you two been up to now?' she asked, bending over Carrie and lifting away a loose dressing to reveal a long gash up the inside of her arm.

'Drove out to dam for swim. Kangaroo,' Carrie said, mumbling through swollen lips. 'Jumped out on the road, swerved to miss it, hit tree.'

Anna checked the admittance sheet the ambulance attendants had left and examined Carrie carefully, alert for signs of internal injury. She explained what she was doing and the samples she'd need for testing, then examined the open wound again.

'Most of the lacerations on your legs will heal well as long as we keep infection at bay, but I'd like to stitch your arm.'

'Will it leave a bad scar?' Carrie asked, and Anna understood the young woman's anxiety.

'Not the way I sew,' she promised, 'though I'm better with sutures than I am with a needle and cotton.'

She sent Elena to get what she needed, and went through to the X-ray room to check on Grace before suturing Carrie's wound.

'How's Carrie?' Grace demanded, with enough anxiety for Anna to realise that the two women, thrown together in unusual circumstances, had become friends.

'She's suffering from shock, of course, and has minor

wounds, but she should be whole again in no time,' Anna said, while her professional self took in Grace's too-pale face and, as Grace was wheeled under an overhead light, a slight difference in pupil size in her eyes.

'Did you hit your head when the car went into the tree?'

Grace frowned at her.

'I don't think so. We weren't travelling fast and I braked when I saw the kangaroo, but as I swerved to avoid it, I must have hit a patch of oil or loose gravel on the road and we just slid sideways off the road and into the tree.'

She pointed to her right ankle.

'The door caved in, which might explain how I hurt my ankle.'

Anna thought about the mechanics of the accident and then eased her fingers into Grace's thick hair, feeling the bones of her skull, seeking any fault or indentation.

'We'll X-ray your skull as well, just to be sure,' she said, when touch alone had failed to find any damage.

The heavy doors to the room slid open and a young woman, clad in cut-off jeans and a singlet top, came in.

'I'm Jillian, I guess you're the new doctor,' she said, coming forward and extending her hand in greeting. 'Now I see you, I can understand why Tom wasn't interested in any of the single women—me included—who threw themselves at him when he arrived in town. He already had you stashed away somewhere.'

Grace protested that he couldn't have known Anna then, but Anna decided to ignore the 'stashed away' comment. She shook Jillian's hand then explained about the skull X-ray.

'I'll just take a look at Grace's ankle,' she added, feeling this was a very odd way to be examining a patient but realising the nurses were probably used to coping on their own when a doctor wasn't immediately available.

The ankle was so swollen a break seemed more likely than a sprain, but Anna was uncertain about protocol. Skull

X-rays were a simple procedure but, with the ankle, did she tell Jillian what angles she wanted or assume the woman would know what was necessary?

'With the ankle, I'll take two lateral views and an angled one,' Jillian said, lifting thick wedges of foam onto the X-ray table ready to hold first Grace's head and then her foot at the appropriate angles. Anna realised the tech knew what she was doing. Better still, the ankle views were the ones Anna would have requested.

Anna left her to it and returned to stitch the long gash in Carrie's arm. Elena was carefully cleaning the lacerations on the patient's legs then spraying them with antiseptic, which made them look ghastly but would stave off infection.

'I'd like you to stay here for a few hours,' Anna told the young woman when the wound was stitched and covered with a sterile dressing. 'Just so we can keep an eye on you.'

Carrie didn't protest, which suggested she was more shaken by the accident than she'd admit.

With one patient settled, Anna returned to the X-ray room where the skull X-rays were ready for her perusal.

'There's no sign of a fracture but we'd need a scan to tell if there's brain damage and we don't have the facilities,' Jillian said, slotting the films into a light-box then looking at them over Anna's shoulder.

'Why are you thinking brain damage?' Anna asked, and Jillian smiled.

'Same reason you asked for skull X-rays,' she said lightly. 'Her pupils are different sizes.'

Anna nodded, and relaxed a little more. She might have the grand title of Medical Superintendent of this hospital, but with staff of the quality of those she'd met so far, her job would be the easy one. These women had the experience of nursing in an isolated town—they would know when a patient could be handled in this hospital and when to either call for help or send the patient on to a larger regional centre.

'OK, let's look at the ankle. That might help us make a decision.'

Jillian put new negatives into the box, then pointed to the hairline mark that indicated a fracture of the lateral malleolus, the lumpy bit of bone on the ankle end of the fibula.

'Do specialists here pin fractures like that?' Anna asked, pointing to the detached but not displaced piece of bone. 'Or do they plaster the ankle and let it heal itself?'

Jillian looked pleased to be consulted.

'With multiple fractures they'd plate and pin fractures of the fibula and with a fracture at the end of the tibia, the medial malleolus, they'd pin, so we automatically send the patient to Rocky. Someone in the family usually drives the patient over, so we're not taking an ambulance off duty, but if we need the ambulance then we let Rocky know and one of their ambulances meets ours halfway. But I think with this, we can plaster it here. A back slab first until the swelling goes down, new X-rays later in the week to check the bone's correctly aligned, then a proper cast.'

Anna nodded her agreement.

'Do you do the casts as well?' she asked, and Jillian beamed at her.

'I love doing them, but if you want a real plaster expert any time, then Jenny, our part-time physio, is really, really good.'

They discussed the back slab, a plaster that would curl around the sole of Grace's foot and up the back of her leg to just below the knee, then be held in place by wide bandages, then Anna left, promising to come back to inspect the finished product.

But the slight difference in the pupil size of Grace's eyes was still bothering her, and she phoned the surgery to ask Peter's advice.

'Did you ask her if it's normal?' he said. 'People can have unequal pupils—or she might have an Adie's pupil, which takes longer to adapt to changes in light. If she has, it could be affected by tiredness.'

It was such a sensible suggestion that Anna felt foolish for having troubled him, but later, when she had both women settled in hospital, and the private session at Peter's surgery was over for the day, Peter assured her it was always better to ask.

'I decided early on—particularly out here where you're on your own a lot of the time—that it was better to appear foolish than to make a mistake. Mistakes happen, I know, but as long as you've covered all the bases, you can't be held responsible.'

Comforted by this practical advice, Anna returned to the hospital. Though Grace had denied any knowledge of uneven pupils, Anna suspected Peter's suggestion of an Adie's pupil was correct as the slightly larger one had diminished in size by the time the plastering was complete. Shining a torch in Grace's eyes proved the point, as one pupil responded more slowly than the other.

When Anna finished with Grace, she checked on Dani. No distracting visitor, but the young woman was fretting about her bed rest.

'It's the goats,' she said. 'I know Tom's been going out to check on them every morning and see to their feed and water, but I can't expect him to keep doing that.'

'And you can't expect to have a healthy baby unless you stay here and rest. It would be different if your husband was at home and could make sure you didn't do anything, but you know as well as I do that if you go home you'll do things. You'll tell yourself you'll just get up for a minute, then you'll see something that needs doing and before you know it, you'll be sick again.'

Dani sighed.

'You're right, of course. I wouldn't stay in bed, but this is so boring!'

'Read a book,' Anna suggested. 'What do you like? Romance? Crime?'

Dani blushed.

'I love romances but Brian teases me about reading them.'

'Well, phooey to him. I can't think of a better or more relaxing way for you to be spending your time here. And it'll stop you fretting about going home. I'll get you some.'

Then, satisfied with Dani's condition, she went on to where Mr Jenks, an elderly man with severe renal failure, was fighting fate.

Knowing she was officially off duty, Anna could spend some time with him, asking him questions about his life as a drover, shifting herds of cattle from one part of the outback to another. His stories fascinated her and she hoped that someone, some time, had written these stories down, because this was part of the outback heritage, and though the huge road trains now shifted cattle, the romance of the drover's life should live on.

Romance!

She chuckled to herself as she left his room. Must have been talking to Dani made her think that way.

'I'm glad you've found something to laugh about!'

The voice startled her and she spun around to find Tom about six inches behind her.

'Do you realise what that car accident means? It means those women won't leave town. They'll have to hang around at least until Grace gets her permanent cast on. Unless…'

He looked hopefully at Anna. 'Unless you could find something seriously wrong with her and send her over to Rocky.'

'Causing further disruption in her life? This is a woman you once loved enough to ask her to marry you,' Anna reminded him, and though he protested about it not quite happening that way, she ignored him and continued, 'And now you want to send her off to a place where she probably knows no one.'

'It's closer to Brisbane where her family live,' Tom pointed out, his blue eyes fixed on Anna's face as if by their force alone he could persuade her to agree with him.

'I thought of that earlier and looked at it on a map,' Anna told him. 'It would be a seven-hour drive from Brisbane to Rockhampton. Hardly what you'd call handy visiting range.'

She stepped aside, meaning to walk past him, but he raised his hand and rested it lightly on her shoulder. The touch, casual though it was, froze her, and she looked questioningly into his eyes.

But there was no answer there, and in the end he shrugged and lifted his hand away, but to Anna it seemed as if a thousand unspoken messages had been transmitted between them in that brief instant.

And she didn't understand any of them!

Tom walked away, and she continued on her final round of the day, winding up in the two-bed room shared by Grace and Carrie.

'You could have gone home—well, back to the motel where you've been staying,' she said to Carrie.

'And leave Grace here on her own? No way! According to the nurses, if she doesn't show any signs of concussion or brain damage during the night, you'll let her out tomorrow, so we'll both go then. In the meantime, I'm working up a nice little article on medical services in the country. Down in the city, we keep hearing about how bad things are out here—tales that doctors won't work here, and how people have to travel hundreds of kilometres to see specialists. But, believe me, Anna, we wouldn't have got this kind of treatment if we'd had our accident in the city.'

'But Grace could have had a scan,' Anna said.

'Maybe—after lying around in A and E for up to four hours. Here we were checked and X-rayed and patched up in no time at all. The hospital is lovely, the staff are wonderful and the food, what we've had of it so far, is terrific.'

Anna was warmed by the praise, though she noticed Grace wasn't equally enthusiastic about country medical services. Or was it simply the doctor providing them that made her scowl?

But ignoring Grace's scowl was easy as Anna accepted Carrie's praise. She might only have been in charge a few days, but already Anna felt a proprietorial interest in the place. She chatted to the two women for a while—it was mostly Carrie who did the talking—all the time aware of the minefield of deception through which she walked, but they didn't prod or probe into her relationship with Tom, and by the time she wished them both goodnight, she was feeling well disposed towards both of them.

It was a strange alliance, she thought as she made her way back to the house. The two of them had been brought together by a shared interest in Tom's love life, yet Anna sensed they'd moved beyond alliance to friendship.

The thought of friendship brought a fleeting pang of envy, but she assured herself she'd soon make friends herself. After all, she hadn't been in town a week yet. There was plenty of time.

But no assurance could banish the thought that there was only one friend she really wanted in this town. And he was the only one she couldn't have.

By the beginning of the following week, Anna had forgotten she'd ever longed to make a friend. Though invitation after invitation had been pressed on her by people she'd met as she'd moved between the hospital and surgery, she was reasonably sure she'd never find time to exchange more than two words, unrelated to work, with the general population of townsfolk, let alone have a social life.

Grace, now sporting a beautiful blue fibreglass cast, and Carrie were once again staying at the motel, though Grace had spent two nights in hospital and had constantly demanded the attendance of her ex-fiancé so Anna had seen more of Tom than she'd wanted.

But although those two had now departed, other people soon took the beds, and the constant flow of admissions and releases kept staff busier than having the same number of long-stay patients. Fortunately, Anna was getting into the rhythm of the coming and going, and adapting to the constant change in her patient population in the hospital, when chickenpox broke out.

Starting at the primary school, it soon swept through the town, keeping both her and Peter busy in the surgery, while two badly affected children had to be admitted to hospital.

'It's impossible, telling the poor things not to scratch,' she said to Jillian who was on night duty on Friday evening when Anna did her late round. 'Bicarbonate of soda baths and soothing lotions will only do so much.'

Jillian was using mouthwash on a cotton bud to soothe the sores in tiny Ginny Parr's mouth, while Maria, the little one's mother, sat helplessly by the bedside.

'At least the sores are crusting now, so it won't be long before she's over the worst,' Anna told her, though looking at the child, so badly affected there was barely a spot the size of a pinhead between her lesions, it didn't seem likely she'd be better any time soon.

Maria, however, found comfort in this. She nodded her head, then said, 'And to think Ryan, who brought it home to all the kids in the first place, only had two spots!'

They talked for a while about the unpredictability of infection, then Anna made her way out of the hospital and across the yard to her home.

Home! Funny how it already feels that way, she thought, though in reality it was so far removed—in physical difference even more than distance—from the home she'd known it may as well have been on the moon.

A message on her answering-machine told her Philip had rung, but as it had been to tell her he was flying to South America for a polo game, she didn't bother trying to contact him on any of the numbers she had for him.

Philip. She conjured up an image of him in her head. He was about the same height as she was, and slight, though with a wiry strength, particularly in his arms and legs, from all the riding and polo playing he had done. She could see him in his polo clothes, and also dressed for work in a beautifully cut three-piece suit. Business clothes suited his elegant figure and the polished sheen of his blond hair.

She tried to see him looking casual—to fit him into a faded blue or checked cotton shirt like most of the locals wore—but it didn't work, and neither did comparisons of classically dressed and professionally coiffed Philip and the thrown-together appearance of Tom.

The two men were so different they might have been from separate species.

The phone rang again and, certain it would be a summons to return to the hospital, she lifted the receiver before the answering-machine came on.

'Hi, it's Tom.'

Ah!

'Over here we usually say hello.'

Ah again.

'You are there, I presume. Are you trying to remember who I am? Big chap. Vet. Little sister called Penny. Actually, it's Penny I'm calling about. She's all over spots and now she tells me there's chickenpox raging through the school. Do we treat chickenpox or let it run its course?'

Damn!

'I'd better take a look at her.' Anna found her voice, and professionalism overcame her reluctance to see the man who was troubling her thoughts. 'Don't bring her out in the cool night air, I'll come to you. I'm on call, but I can put any calls through to my mobile.'

'Thanks.'

The click told her he'd hung up. Perhaps he wasn't any more eager to talk to her than she was to talk to him.

She drove the roundabout route to Tom's place, thinking she really should find time to explore her surroundings— she could probably have walked across more quickly—and pulled up behind a vaguely familiar car.

Tom came out of the shadows on the veranda, sprang down to the ground and walked swiftly towards her. He stopped an arm's length away, then reached out and drew her close.

'What I didn't tell you is that I have more house guests. Only one more in total as Jim moved out as soon as the invasion happened, but Grace and Carrie are staying here. Just until Monday when they're both flying back to Brisbane. It seems the motel had a long-held booking for their rooms and there was no other accommodation available in town.'

Anna realised he was holding her like this while he explained to give the impression of a lovers' greeting, but the proximity was disturbing—no, more than disturbing, it was positively volcanic.

And while she knew she should make some light-hearted remark about his inability to say no, her reaction to his touch had stopped her mouth working.

Damn, she thought again, then Tom bent his head and kissed her.

She knew it was for show—an act for unseen watchers either on the veranda or inside the house—but her heart didn't understand and skittered into idiocy, while the pal-

pitations from it froze her lungs, making the simple act of
drawing breath impossible.

'I—I'd better take a look at Penny,' she eventually managed to stutter, and Tom, apparently more able than her to
cope with pretend kisses, simple nodded his agreement,
and with his arm slung casually across her shoulders
guided her inside.

'Oh, you poor thing!'

The sight of Penny's spotted face brought her back
down to earth with a thud, though as yet the attack looked
like a mild one.

'I don't feel sick,' Penny told her cheerfully. 'And I
know what it is because half the school's got it. It's just
Tom fussing, making you come around.'

She grinned at Anna. 'And he might have wanted an
excuse to get away from his other visitors as well,' she
whispered, as Anna came closer and bent to lift Penny's
wrist and feel her skin for heat.

Anna checked her out and confirmed Penny's guess that
she wasn't too bad, then agreed she'd better stay off school
until the spots were gone.

'It's a pity, actually, as I was enjoying it.' Penny's
youthful candour made Anna smile. 'I mean, I don't really
belong in the class so no one expects me to do any work,
and I've made some fabulous friends.'

Again the issue of friendship raised its head, and again
Anna was aware of the emptiness inside her where friends
should be. Or *a* friend, at least.

'Want to see the colt?'

Tom's head poked around the doorway in a manner that
was almost familiar.

'I thought you said Jim had moved on,' Anna reminded
him, mainly because, though she really did want to see the
colt, she wasn't sure seeing it with Tom was such a good
idea.

'He has.' Tom smiled at her then winked at Penny.

'Couldn't stand all the women round the place. But he's still in town—found a friend at the pub and shifted in with him until Felicity and Frank are ready to travel.'

'Frank? He called that beautiful animal Frank?' Disbelief made Anna forget about friends—though they were becoming a recurring theme—and good or bad ideas.

'*I* called him Frank,' Penny said with immense dignity. 'And if you think about it, it's a great name. It's Jim's father's name for a start, and it also means open and honest and Jim says that's what draught horses are—honest toilers.'

Anna offered a suitably chastened apology then, with a little more urging from Penny, agreed to go and see the colt.

'I'll come back to check on you some time tomorrow,' she told her patient, then she joined Tom in the doorway.

For a moment she hesitated, held back by a reluctance that was almost fearful in its intensity, but then the familiar gesture, a touch of his hand on her shoulder, and she went as docilely as a child.

Or a lamb to the slaughter! the reluctant bit suggested.

But the colt was truly beautiful, standing straight and tall beside his mother.

'He looks as if he's doubled his size,' Anna said, amazed to see the difference in so short a time.

'He probably has—Jim could tell you. I swear he measures him three times a day.'

Anna reached out over the half-door of the stall and ran her hand over the still rough coat of the foal.

'He's beautiful!' she murmured, and turned, right into Tom's arms.

'So are you,' he said, shaking his head as if he couldn't quite take in what was happening.

Which made two of them, but Anna didn't turn away. In fact, as he lowered his head, aiming his lips unmistakably towards hers, she shifted so she could meet him halfway.

And this time there was no margin of pretence. This time it was a kiss between two adults who were finally giving in to an attraction that had sizzled between them from their first meeting.

Anna felt heat rising in her body, felt more heat as Tom's hands seem to weld themselves to her shoulders. Her knees shook as tremors of desire swept over her, but nothing could make her shift her lips from Tom's or from the sweet fulfilment and even sweeter promise of that kiss.

Eventually the need to breathe broke them apart, but Tom wouldn't let her escape, cradling her in his strong arms, pressing her body against his so she could feel her flesh learning the shape and texture of his as if it needed the pattern of it to be imprinted on its cells.

'This can't happen,' she said at last. 'It won't work. I'm engaged to Philip and…'

She hesitated as all the threads linking her to Philip and to her future with him took a stranglehold on her, coiling around her neck and shoulders, weighing as heavily as the harness and yoke of an ox.

'I was engaged to Grace once. Engagements can be broken,' Tom said, but even before he heard his own words he felt an overwhelming sadness. He remembered how he'd felt when Grace had broken off their engagement, how betrayed and devastated that a woman he'd thought he loved could let him down in such a way.

Did he really want to become involved with a woman who would break such a commitment—not to him but to some other poor bloke?

He was still considering this when Anna spoke.

'Not this engagement,' she said quietly, looking up into his eyes. 'It's too complicated, Tom. I owe him so much, and on top of that there are other people to consider. My father, my cousin, even my best friend work for Philip, my parents live in a house on his estate. We're not married yet, but our lives are inextricably linked. They have been for years.'

She backed out of the circle of Tom's arms and walked away, head bowed so the three-quarter moon shone on her blonde hair, turning it to a shimmering silver.

He watched her go, his mind processing the information she'd just given him, adding more snippets of knowledge he'd gleaned from Penny's chatter. But while he understood the concepts that tied her to her fiancé—duty, obligation, family—and applauded them, there was one glaring omission from the explanation.

She hadn't mentioned love...

Anna was almost at the car when the tinkling melody of her mobile stopped her.

Hopefully it was just the hospital wanting her back there, because she wasn't sure she was emotionally capable of dealing with too huge a crisis. Not while her reactions to Tom Fleming were turning her inside out...

'My husband's caught his hand in the grain auger and it's almost off. I can't get the ambulance, can you come?'

While part of Anna's mind wondered what a grain auger was, the other part concentrated on more practical matters. Emotional confusion was forgotten as training and professionalism concentrated her mind on the man who needed her help.

'Who is it calling, and where do you live?' she asked, heading for her car and a pen to write down the information.

'It's Mavis Cullen and we're out at the Sixteen Mile. Have you been out here? You take the Three Gorges Road, the property's called Havemore. The turn-off's about twenty kilometres along on the left, then you follow the dirt road to the State Forest sign and turn right across the grid just past it.'

'Havemore, Three Gorges Road, twenty k's,' Anna repeated, hoping she'd remember the directions without writing them down, because right now the patient's condition was of prime importance.

'Where's your husband now?'

'He's in the shed. I didn't know how to get his hand out. I put a blanket round him and packed ice around his hand. You might have to cut it off.'

Her voice faltered as she added this desperate possibility, and Anna felt her stomach somersault as she considered such an amputation. Tom had crossed to stand beside her and must have heard the conversation for he rested his hand on her shoulder as if to offer his physical support.

'Do you have a Royal Flying Doctor Service emergency kit?' Anna asked, thinking of the morphine that was part of the supplies.

'No, we've not been here very long, and Kevin thought we were too close to town to qualify.'

She sounded as if not having one was a problem, and Anna hastened to reassure her.

'That's OK. You could give him a drink—not alcohol, but something warm and sweet,' Anna said. 'I'm on my way but I'll have my mobile with me so phone me if you need me.'

'Your mobile won't work out there, but it's the assurance that counts.' Tom's voice startled her out of terrifying thoughts of what might lie ahead. 'Now, hop in and I'll drive you out there. I know the way and know the road. That'll save at least fifteen minutes. You can phone Penny...' he rattled off his phone number '...and tell her what's happening and that I'll be home in a couple of hours.'

Anna started to protest, then realised the fifteen minutes they'd save might make all the difference in saving Mr Cullen's hand.

She climbed into the passenger seat of her car and

phoned Penny, explaining why Tom was driving her and that he'd be in touch from the Cullens' house.

'What's a grain auger?' Anna asked, when she'd finished her conversation with Penny.

'It's a long metal spiral thingy inside a metal tube—like a long carpenter's drill. It works on a motor, and as it turns it lifts grain from one place to another—perhaps from a bin to a silo, or from a silo to a feed drum.'

'Oh!'

The thought of a man's hand caught in such a device was horrifying.

'I think you'd be looking at crush injuries, and possibly partial amputation.'

Anna tried to picture the metal spiral turning within its tube, pulling the man's hand up with it.

'Crush injuries might be good,' she said, more to herself than to Tom. 'At least if it's wedged tight, it might shut off any damaged blood vessels so there's less danger of a bad haemorrhage.'

'Except that he's a farmer and needs two hands, preferably two that work.'

'And with crush injuries, the damage might be irreversible.' Anna admitted the possibility, her voice husky with concern. Then her mind returned to the problem of the auger.

'Does it have a reverse—this machine? Do you know? Could we make it run backwards and release the hand?'

'I imagine if it does, Kevin will have tried that,' Tom said, peering ahead to find the turn-off they needed.

'So we'd have to cut the metal sleeve to get his hand out—and somehow do it so we don't injure him more. Perhaps above or below where it's caught...'

Tom glanced towards his passenger. He could only see her profile as she looked out into the night, but he could hear her frown in the worried tone of voice and could almost follow her thought processes as she considered what lay ahead of her. For a city girl, she was remarkably cool in emergencies—and, remembering the foaling, remarkably unfazed by the messy aspects of country life.

A tiny spark of what-could-be flared briefly in his heart, but his mind reminded him that anyone could handle outback life if they knew it was only for a short time.

They reached the State Forest sign and he swung in over the grid, slowing down as the road narrowed to little more than a track between the crowding rosewood trees.

'Bloody stupid, that's what I am.'

Kevin Cullen greeted them with this growled opinion. He was sitting on a box in an open-fronted shelter, his right arm disappearing up a rusty orange tube.

'If anyone knows not to put his hand near a bloody grain auger, it's me. Didn't I see my dad lose his fingers this way? Now I've gone and done it!'

Anna, who'd introduced herself when they'd arrived, was bent over the man, checking the condition of the rest of his body, seemingly oblivious to the man's grumbling about his own stupidity.

'Do you know what part of your hand is trapped, and where in the machine it's stuck?'

Kevin tapped the machine about fifteen centimetres from the bottom.

'The auger picked up four fingers and they're squashed against the outside tube. They must still be attached to my hand or I'd be able to get the damn thing out. I told Mavis to reverse it but it stopped when I got caught and she couldn't start it up again. Reckon I burnt the motor out.'

'Perhaps it's just as well,' Anna told him. 'Reversing it might have finished off the job of amputating your fingers.'

She paused and looked around the shed, her eyes settling on a workbench in one corner.

'Do you have an angle-grinder?'

'What would a pretty thing like you know about angle-grinders?' Kevin asked, and, though Tom was interested in the answer, he left the pair of them to cross to the bench. There was an angle-grinder, but not a nifty little handyman's machine. It was so big that putting its blade anywhere near the auger would risk taking off Kevin's whole hand.

'We'll have to use it.'

Anna's determined decision made him turn. She was right behind him, eyeing the power-tool with professional approval. 'We'll cut through the other side from the bottom up past where his hand's caught then pry the cylinder open.'

'With what?' Tom demanded, plugging in the lead and following her back towards her patient.

'I don't know—a jack if necessary. But you two men are the outback guys—you should be able to think of something.'

Tom wasn't sure why Anna's confidence was disconcerting, but realised now wasn't the time to think about why a woman who looked like her would know about power-tools. Now he had to concentrate on cutting Tom free, and think about how they could pry the metal apart.

'I've got a small clamp over there—you can put it in the split and wind it out rather than in,' Kevin offered, apparently unperturbed by the thought of someone wielding an angle-grinder so close to his injured hand.

Anna fetched the clamp—more familiarity with tools—then turned her attention to the patient.

'It's going to hurt like hell the moment Tom releases the pressure. In fact, the vibration of the blade cutting will hurt first. I'm going to give you some morphine and it will make you woozy so Mavis and I will hold you steady. I don't want you keeling over and putting more stress on your hand.'

She injected the painkiller then organised Mavis into position. Tom watched with a surprise bordering on disbelief. He knew doctors could cope with most situations—

but a city doctor behaving so calmly in this bizarre accident? A city doctor who looked more like a model than a medical expert?

It was even stranger than her knowledge of power-tools.

Anna braced herself against her patient, and nodded to Tom to start cutting. Her stomach churned with anxiety and she hoped Kevin couldn't feel the tremors of fear running through her body. She knew the most important thing in any emergency was to remain calm, so had made a supreme effort to project an unruffled demeanour, as well appear totally confident in her actions and speech.

Had it worked?

And would they be able to cut Kevin free?

She had no idea but knew they had to try.

The ambulance arrived as Tom was prying the metal cylinder open. Fortunately, Tom had passed out by now, so was unaware of the problems they were having. The ambulance carried small implements modelled on the larger 'jaws of life' used to pry open car bodies to release trapped patients. These worked well, and within minutes of the ambulance's arrival Anna had Tom's hand resting on a sterile dressing while she examined the damage.

'He needs an expert hand surgeon to put it back together,' she said, wrapping it loosely. 'I'll check if there's one in Rocky, but otherwise he'll have to go to Brisbane. Maybe Brisbane would be better anyway, which means a plane retrieval rather than the helicopter.'

She didn't realise she was thinking aloud until the ambulance driver offered to get on the radio straight away to organise it.

Anna nodded, but absent-mindedly. The palm and fingers of Kevin's hand were badly crushed and it would be a delicate job, piecing together injured nerves and tendons, but right now it was the bleeding that worried her most.

'He's always been a bleeder,' Mavis said, picking up on

Anna's anxiety. 'Not one of those haemophiliacs, but says he's close, he bleeds that much!'

Anna nodded. At the moment she was keeping a gentle pressure on his wrist and it was enough to slow the flow, but for transport?

The ambulance men lifted the supine patient onto a stretcher and Anna, still holding his wrist, turned to Tom.

'I need to go back with him. Do you mind bringing my car back to the hospital?'

He was over by the bench, where he'd restored the angle-grinder and clamp to their rightful positions.

'Of course not,' he said. 'You go, I'll stay with Mavis and see what she wants to do.'

'I've got no choice,' Mavis said. 'I've got to stay here. Kevin'll understand. He knows, with the drought, the animals have to be fed.'

She sounded brave but despairing, but when Anna turned to her, asking her to pack a small bag for Kevin and to include any medication he was on, she hurried away, no doubt grateful to have something to do to take her mind off her injured husband's imminent departure.

Tom joined Anna who was now examining Kevin's hand again, though this time at the rear of the ambulance.

'The spotlights at the back give better light than we had in the shed,' she explained, using a probe to pick a grain of wheat from the lacerated palm.

'Do you tie off those blood vessels?' he asked, as the oozing blood obliterated everything.

'I don't want to,' Anna told him. 'Not if I can avoid it. The more I fiddle with the things the more chance there is of doing further damage to nerve fibres that run alongside or underneath them. It's easier to replace blood,' she added, nodding to the bottle of fluid already hooked up to a vein in Kevin's good arm. 'It's just a matter of controlling the bleeding without compromising blood delivery to the uninjured part of his hand.'

'If there is such a place,' Tom said, doubtfully eyeing the mangled flesh.

'There is,' Anna said stoutly. 'This man's a farmer and needs both his hands!'

She rewrapped the injured hand carefully, then stepped back as the ambulance men loaded her patient into the vehicle.

'You go, I'll bring the bag Mavis is packing,' Tom said, then he touched her lightly on the shoulder, bringing a wave of awareness washing across her skin. 'I'll see you at home.'

The final words brought another wave, this time along her nerves.

Her only hope of retaining any sanity lay in avoiding him—at all times, at all costs…

CHAPTER SEVEN

AVOIDING Tom might have become essential now, but right when the excuse of learning her new job would have proved useful, work slackened off. Suddenly, no one was getting ill, or perhaps it was simply that Anna had become familiar with the routine and better at handling the interruptions in her daily schedule.

As if in celebration of this lull, the news from Brisbane was good. Microsurgeons had pieced together Kevin's hand and though he was still hospitalised down there and would stay for intensive physiotherapy once the surgical scars healed, the surgeons were optimistic he would regain ninety per cent function.

Anna had even had time to go out and visit Mavis, wanting to explain in person what was going on and how Kevin was responding to the surgery.

But even with this and other home visits to patients, Anna now had time on her hands, so when Beryl Martin, the head of the local shire council, asked her to open the Merriwee Art Show the following Saturday night, she agreed.

'The opening is at seven-thirty,' Beryl explained, capturing Anna in the corridor outside the hospital kitchen. 'But I've asked a few people to an early buffet dinner at my place first, so come along there at six. You remember how to get there?'

Anna nodded. She'd met Beryl several times, and had been to her house to discuss the arrangement by which the hospital kitchen supplied the meals for the volunteer meals-on-wheels service—one of many services in the town headed by the seemingly tireless and indomitable Beryl.

'So, although opening the local art show might not rate right up there with playing polo against royalty,' Anna said to Philip when he phoned on Saturday afternoon, 'at least tonight I'll meet some of the locals socially, rather than professionally.'

'You've not met any of them yet?' Even over thousands of kilometres of radio waves Philip could sound incredulous. 'What on earth have you been doing in your spare time?'

'What spare time?' Anna retorted, but Philip was already telling her about the friends he'd caught up with at the opera in Milan when he'd flown in for business and been fortunate enough to get tickets.

He's always fortunate enough to get tickets, Anna thought to herself, then realised that even thinking such a thing was bitchy, so she made up for it with noises of appreciation and amazement as Philip talked on.

And on!

It meant she had to rush through her shower, with no time to wash her hair, and she was left with little time after showering to decide what one wore to open an art show in Merriwee.

She hadn't realised just what a problem clothes could be until she'd arrived in Merriwee. Warnings of the heat had prompted her to pack miniskirts and skimpy tops, but she'd soon learnt they weren't the kind of clothes the locals expected their doctor to wear. At work, her white coats were long enough to cover up the fact her skirts were too short, and, in spite of over 40-degree heat, she usually wore jeans when she went uptown.

But to open an art show?

'Nothing too flashy, I assume,' she said, staring into the wardrobe though she knew there was nothing even approaching the calf-length linen skirts and shirt-style tops most of the older local women wore.

'But not too dressy. The women here are stylish, but generally conservative where clothes are concerned.'

The cat, no doubt hearing Anna's voice and perhaps assuming her company was Tom, appeared and slid into the open wardrobe.

'Don't take up residence in there,' Anna warned, but the movement of the animal had shifted things slightly and she noticed a green linen shift she'd bought while staying with friends in Melbourne.

She pulled it out and slipped it on, smiling because it was a dress that, right from the first time she'd seen it, she'd liked for its elegant simplicity. Best of all, it came down to her knees—not calf-length, but better than mid-thigh!

Brushing her hair back, she used clips to hold it behind her ears, an easy way to make it look as if she'd made an effort with it. Though now, of course, she needed earrings.

She flicked through the mess in her jewellery case, glad Philip, who was always telling her she should take better care of the jewels he gave her, wasn't here to see the disorder. Not that she could wear anything Philip had given her to open an art show in Merriwee. A big diamond on an engagement ring was one thing—diamond drop earrings that reached to her shoulders were quite another.

Fishing around, she found the tiny diamond studs her parents had given her for her twenty-first birthday and, removing the plain gold studs she usually wore, she slid the diamond ones into her ears.

'A bit of make-up and we're done,' she told Cassie, who had finished exploring the wardrobe and was now sitting on the bed. But when Anna whirled in front of the cat for final approval, all she got was the narrow-eyed stare.

'Well, rats to you!' Anna said, and walked out of the room, though she soon returned, searching through her usual handbag for her mobile and transferring it to the small green bag she was carrying tonight. Peter was on call, but she didn't like being completely out of touch.

She reached Beryl's place only slightly late, then was made later by having to circle the block in search of a parking space. Parking problems in Merriwee? Had Beryl invited the entire town to dinner before the show?

Huffing from her fast walk, Anna climbed the front steps to the wide veranda of the high-set house. Social chat and laughter, loud above music, masked Anna's knock, but someone passing across the long hallway that led to the back of the house took pity on her and ushered her inside.

'You can't stand on ceremony out here,' the middle-aged man said. 'Just knock and walk right in. That's the rule in most of the places in Merriwee, and on the country properties, too. Out on a property, the missus might be teaching her kids and have School of the Air going. She can't be getting up to the door every time someone knocks, now, can she?'

The stranger had his hand on Anna's back, guiding her forward in a way that was becoming familiar. Though not as familiar as the first face she saw. Inevitable, really, as he stood head and shoulders above the two women to whom he was talking.

Tom was wearing a blue shirt again, but tonight the sleeves were rolled down, cuffs and collar buttoned and a neatly knotted but conservatively striped tie had been added to what was almost a uniform for him. Yet, even with the tie, he still looked every bit an outdoorsman, a man who'd be as much at home in the vast paddocks of the outback as the cattlemen he served.

'Ah, there's your man, he'll take care of you now,' Anna's guide announced, steering her towards Tom. 'Beryl's somewhere around. She'll catch up with you.'

The good Samaritan beat a hasty retreat, and the two

women who'd been with Tom also disappeared, leaving her alone with the man she most wanted to avoid.

And her reaction to being alone with him reminded her of why avoidance was a necessity. Though still in the middle of a noisy gathering, they could have been on a desert island for all the impact the fellow guests were having on Anna. Her entire body was alert to Tom's presence, as if being near him was akin to being plugged into a high-voltage power line. It hummed and shivered, while her mind, maybe shocked by the power surge, went totally blank.

'They're being kind. Giving us time to greet each other in relative privacy,' Tom explained. His large hand touched her lightly on the arm, and his blue eyes seemed to be photographing her.

The touch helped, earthing her energised body, but still no words would come and all she could do was look up into his face, absorbing the rugged lines of nose, cheek-bones, chin, and catching a glimpse of a strange light in the mesmerising blue eyes.

'You look very beautiful,' he said quietly, and Anna felt the kind of blush she'd thought she'd left behind in adolescence climb up her neck and into her cheeks.

'I didn't know you'd be here,' she said, stumbling over the words in her haste to appear cool and in control while her body, thrumming with the charge, was anything but cool, and her mind far from in control.

Tom smiled. 'I'll always be here,' he said, and for a moment she thought he was making a promise and her silly heart jittered with excitement. Then he continued, 'Thanks to Penny and Bob, not to mention Barb at the supermarket, the whole town now thinks we're engaged, so anyone inviting either of us anywhere will naturally invite the other.'

'Oh!'

It wasn't a particularly adequate response but it was all

Anna could manage right then. The thought of being socially linked to Tom for the rest of her stay in Merriwee was too overwhelming to take in all at once. Especially as the part of her that wasn't in control was acting all excited over the prospect.

'How's Penny?' she asked, seeking a conversational escape from personal matters.

'Spots fading nicely. The only problem was restraining Pat from flying up to nurse her.'

He rubbed the back of his neck as if in physical pain, and added, 'I don't know—I come up here to escape a houseful of women and suddenly I've got three in residence and another threatening.'

Anna felt a fleeting sympathy for his predicament, then remembered an earlier conversation.

'You've three in residence? I thought you said Grace and Carrie were leaving on Monday.'

Tom nodded gloomily.

'They were, but apparently Carrie's decided she's in love with Bob so wants to stay a little longer. She wangled some extra time from her editor. And Grace tells me she has six weeks' leave from work so might as well stay on until her cast's off. I think she realises that if she went home she'd have to look after herself, whereas here she's got Carrie to fuss over her.'

'Here in Merriwee, or here at your place?' Anna asked, feeling squidgy in the stomach although it was none of her business where Grace stayed.

'The latter!' Tom admitted, becoming even gloomier.

'But the motel can't still be booked out!' Anna protested.

Tom shrugged his impossibly broad shoulders and now the gloom on his face segued into embarrassment.

'I can't just turn them out!' he said. 'You know how big that house is. I can't say I don't have room for them. And, to a certain extent, it makes things a bit easier for me because of Pen. I know she's old enough to leave on her own if I'm called out at night, but I still don't like it. At least now I don't worry about her the whole time.'

'That's an excuse,' Anna told him, then she shook her head in amazement. 'You really can't say no, can you? Penny told me that, and I didn't believe it.'

'I can so say no,' Tom retorted, then heard how childish he'd sounded and smiled. But he backed up his denial with an example. 'Just the other day, Phil Webster out at Longalook wanted me to go out and spay some young heifers at night, just because he had them in the yard and it suited him to get them done then. I said no to him.'

The look Anna gave him was downright disbelieving.

'Probably because you knew you could muck up the job. I imagine it's difficult at the best of times, but at night, even under the best of lights, it would be near impossible.'

She was so beautiful, and arguing so earnestly with him, he wanted to keep looking at her—talking to her.

Even arguing.

'And what would you know about spaying cattle?' he asked, and was rewarded with one of the flashing smiles that made his heart thunder in his chest in a way that told him all the red alert warnings in his head hadn't prevented him from falling in love with this woman.

'Not a lot,' she admitted, and seemed about to say something else when Beryl bore down on them.

'Come on, you two, you've had enough time together. Now I want to introduce Anna to a few people.'

She took Anna's arm, then turned back to Tom.

'And I expect you to mingle,' she told him. 'There are a couple of new forestry rangers here—they're over in the corner near the bar. Start with them.'

'He's so good,' Beryl said to Anna, 'at talking to people, especially women, of course, and making them relax. But, then, you'd know that.'

She squeezed Anna's arm.

'You're a very lucky girl, but I suppose you know that too. Not that he's not lucky to have a beautiful fiancée like you. Now, how did you meet? Someone said it was over the internet.'

Fortunately, before Anna had to reply they joined a group of businesspeople, and Beryl was too busy introducing Anna to demand an answer to her question.

Anna acknowledged the introductions and stayed to chat, moving on as one person or another offered to introduce her to more people. Someone escorted her to the buffet where she filled her plate with an assortment of meat and salad, someone else brought her a drink—a punch of some kind that looked peculiar, being pink, but tasted absolutely delicious.

But all the while part of her mind—and most of her body—was attuned to Tom's presence. Every time she turned her head she'd catch a glimpse of him, and more often than not find him turned her way. He'd wink, or smile, and Anna would desperately rub her thumb against the gold of Philip's ring and remind herself it was all pretence.

'You did that brilliantly,' he said, materialising by her side only minutes after she'd declared the art show open. 'And now we've both done our duty and been suitably social, the locals will expect us to spend some time together.'

Anna studied his face, trying to read his mood. The words were light-hearted enough but she sensed more behind them. Sensed that spending more time with him, even in a crowd, wasn't a good idea.

'I think we should break off this engagement,' she told him. They were standing in front of a painting of a bullock team, and she studied the play of light on the animals' coats so she didn't have to look at him.

'With Grace still here—and Carrie?' he said, making it sound like the worst idea since the atom bomb.

'It's deceitful,' Anna persisted. 'And the townspeople are so kind and welcoming, I hate deceiving them.'

'We could make it real,' Tom suggested, shocking Anna so much she forgot the artist's masterly way with light and turned towards him.

'We can't!' she said, using as much vehemence as would fit into a whisper. 'In case you've forgotten, I'm already engaged. To Philip!'

'Well, that's his problem,' Tom told her, the twinkle that always disconcerted her sparkling in his eyes. 'For letting you out of his sight. The man must be mad! Believe me, Anna Talbot, if I really was engaged to you, I wouldn't want to be parted from you for a minute.'

'He did it for me—because I wanted so badly to come,' Anna told him, anxious to defend her absent fiancé. 'Anyway,' she added defiantly, 'it won't be for the whole six months—he'll come and visit when next he's in Australia.'

Tom's gleeful smile told her she'd said the wrong thing, and he didn't leave her in doubt about it for long.

'Well, that *will* be fun!' he said, taking her left hand and lifting it as if to examine her engagement ring. 'The doctor's two fiancés! The town will love it!'

In spite of the heat generated by Tom's clasp on her hand, Anna shivered. She tried to think but the enormity of what Tom had just pointed out was too big to comprehend.

Why hadn't *she* thought of it? Thought of what would happen when Philip came?

He'd understand, of course, the pretend engagement situation. Once she'd explained...

Yes, of course he would...

But the townsfolk?

'Oh, hell!' she said, then, to make matters worse, when Tom put his arm around her—in a comforting manner, nothing more—she actually felt like snuggling up against him and letting him take care of all her problems.

The country air must be addling your brain, she told herself, but it didn't stop a little snuggle up against his solid, strong, oh, so desirable body.

Heavens! Had she really thought desirable? Surely that should have been reliable...

'How do you know so much about power-tools?'

The question, coming when she was thinking about desirable—or reliable—bodies, threw her completely. She stared at Tom, trying to make sense of the shift in conversation.

'Out at the Cullens' place,' he prompted. 'You knew an angle-grinder from a chainsaw—most women wouldn't. I've been wanting to ask ever since that night.'

Thinking of how she knew an angle-grinder from a chainsaw prompted Anna to smile.

'My dad,' she said softly. 'He was a power-tool junkie and I guess, because he didn't have a son, he had to make do with sharing his toys with me.'

Tom returned her smile with one that started thoughts of desire if not desirability.

'I'm sure he didn't mind making do with you,' he murmured, making it sound like the most romantic compliment Anna had ever been paid.

A loud wailing siren stopped her wayward thoughts, and most of the conversation in the room.

'Damn!' Tom said. 'Hope it's not a bad one.'

Then, to Anna's astonishment, he bent his head and kissed her swiftly on the lips.

'Till next time, sweetheart,' he said putting on a gruff American accent, then he strode away.

Anna turned to watch him go, totally flummoxed by his behaviour. Until she realised other men and a couple of women were also heading for the door, while somewhere in the dark night outside the siren continued its noise.

'What's happening?' she asked, turning to a woman who was looking anxiously out into the night.

'It's the fire siren,' the woman explained. 'I suppose we should have expected it, with the wind that's got up.'

Anna understood the fire siren part of this explanation, but not why so many people had left the room.

'Is the town in danger?' she asked, thinking she'd better get back to the hospital in case she was needed there.

'I wouldn't think so. Most of the fires are out on properties, or on forestry land that's leased to local farmers. Though a couple of years ago a big one swept close to town. The place was grey with ash for days.'

'But why did the people leave?' Anna asked.

The woman turned towards her.

'They're on duty,' she said, as if that explained everything, then, perhaps seeing Anna's blank look, she continued, 'We don't have a regular fire brigade in town, only the volunteer fire service. It's the same in nearly all country towns. Most of the younger men and a lot of the younger women are volunteers. They train on certain nights, they have a proper fire engine and all the right gear, and they're rostered on and off duty. So when the siren sounds, if you're on call, you go, no matter where you are or what you're doing. Your Tom, he's usually on call at night because during the day he mightn't be able to leave his job. Not if he's operating on someone's dog, or something.'

Anna nodded, but didn't—couldn't—speak. She understood the situation now, but anxiety for Tom, heading out into the bush to fight a raging fire, had tied her tongue in knots.

'Most people will go home now,' her kindly informant said. 'We'll wait there for news. If it's a big fire and the men will be out for a while, a group of women—we're on a roster, too—will make sandwiches and fill Thermoses with coffee to take out to the firefighters, and we keep food and drinks going back at the community hall for when a crew comes in for a break.'

'Thank you for explaining,' Anna managed to say, though she hadn't liked any of the information.

She found Beryl, said goodbye and joined the exodus. As she walked around the corner towards where her car was parked, her mobile rang. Pleased it hadn't happened while she'd been opening the show, she pulled it out of her handbag and answered it.

'Peter here, Anna. You heard the sirens? I don't know if Paul explained the drill before he left but, if not, that was a fire siren and our job is to be prepared for any casualties that might come in. If it's bad, we set up a first-aid post closer to the scene, but until we hear the extent of it, the ambulance and the hospital just stay on alert.'

'I'm on my way back now,' Anna told him. 'Should I wait at the hospital or at the house?'

'Go home, but be prepared to be called in,' Peter said. 'The nursing staff know the ropes. They'll have everything we need on hand should things turn nasty.'

Anna thanked him, though she hated the information he'd delivered even more than the things she'd heard earlier. 'Things turn nasty'—what had he meant by that?

'Fires can turn around and trap the firefighters,' Jess told her when she arrived at the hospital. Peter might have said to wait at home, but she knew she was too anxious to sit there doing nothing, so had come to the hospital instead. 'The wind gusts are so unpredictable, and because of the high oil content in eucalypt leaves, bush fires travel through the tops of trees, leaping from one tree to another, even across roads and fire-breaks.'

Anna realised that the more she asked—or the more she learnt—the worse she felt, as anxiety for Tom now knotted her intestines as well as her tongue.

She walked through into the small A and E room, and saw packaged sterile dressings and bandages laid out on trolleys, bottles of saline for washing wounds, bags of fluid already hanging on drip stands.

'Just pray we don't need any of it,' Jess, who'd followed her, said quietly.

'Do you often need it?' Anna asked, though it was a fifty-fifty chance she'd not like the answer.

'Not often,' Jess replied.

Ah, the relief—until Jess spoke again.

'Though when we do need it, it's usually bad. Three Gorges lost three of their volunteers a couple of years ago. Of course, down there, the fires race through the gorges, and if they turn, the men are more easily trapped.'

Thinking there could be no worse way to die, Anna shuddered, and though Jess was quick to point out that more people were murdered in the city each year than killed as volunteer firefighters, Anna wasn't comforted.

She checked on all three of the patients she had in hospital, sat in the office and did some paperwork, walked through the dim corridors a few more times, and finally, after Jess pointed out a fire could burn for days and Anna wouldn't be much use to anyone if she didn't get some sleep, she went back to the house.

The phone was ringing as she walked in, and she answered it to hear a suspicious sniff, then Penny's voice.

'I heard the fire siren. Was Tom on call?'

'Yes, he was, Penny,' Anna said. 'Are you OK? Are Grace and Carrie there?'

Another sniff.

'No. They went to Bob's.'

Anna's heart went out to the young girl. She might act like thirteen going on thirty, but she was still a child—and a child who'd already lost her father and would be doubly fearful of losing a beloved brother.

'I'll come right over. I'll bring night things. The hospital can phone me on my mobile if they need me.'

A whispered 'Thank you' then the click of the receiver being replaced.

Poor kid.

Anna grabbed her nightdress and a toilet bag, then, deciding she'd better not turn up at the hospital to tend burn victims in her best green dress, she added her jeans and a T-shirt to the pile. She thrust everything into a bag, checked Cass had water, then left, driving swiftly through the night.

Penny was waiting on the veranda.

'I'm really all right,' she told Anna, greeting her with a hug.

'I know you are.' Anna hugged her back, but as she clasped the girl's solid body against her, she felt a sob escape, and knew tears would follow.

'Let's sit down—out here would be nice,' she suggested, knowing Penny might be embarrassed to be seen crying. 'We can look at the stars, talk if you want to, or just sit if that's what you'd prefer.'

They shuffled over to the steps and sat down on the top one. The smell of smoke drifted through the air and, sniffing it, Penny began to cry again.

'I talked to a lot of people after the sirens went off,' Anna said, hoping to reassure her friend. 'And they all said the firefighters know what they're doing. At the hospital I heard it wasn't a bad fire—just a grass fire. And there's practically no wind—that's a good thing, isn't it?'

Penny nodded, but continued to cry.

'There's something else bothering you, isn't there, pet?' Anna said, tightening her arm around Penny's shoulders.

'Not really.' The words were muffled by a handkerchief. 'It's just that everything keeps changing. Mum got married and Patience went off to university and Tom came up here.'

Anna let her talk, encouraging her when the tidal wave of sorrow seemed to dry up, knowing it was better for Penny to let it all out. Then she probed, asking questions that would make Penny find the answers to her own dilemma. Yes, she liked Keith, yes, she had good friends of her own at home, no, living here with Tom was nice now, but she wouldn't want to stay for ever.

And slowly the girl calmed down, then promptly fell asleep against Anna's shoulder. She was wondering whether to let Penny sleep for a while, or wake her and guide her back to bed, when car headlights pinned the pair of them like a spotlight hitting actors on a stage.

The lights went off, and within seconds Tom was by her side.

'What's wrong with Penny?' he demanded, though quietly so he must have seen his sister was asleep.

'She was upset—over you being out at the fire and then a lot of other stuff came out. I think she's probably still physically weakened by the chickenpox, and she's been through a lot of emotional change this year as well.'

She couldn't see Tom's frown, but sensed it. Sensed also his unspoken question—Why the hell's she telling you this?

'She phoned me to ask if you'd gone to the fire, and sounded upset so I came over.'

Tom dropped down onto the step beside them and touched first his sister, then Anna lightly on the hair.

'The fire's out—it was only a minor blaze. But Penny? She sounded upset and you came over?'

Anna nodded, though sitting next to Tom in the admittedly smoky moonlight wasn't a particularly good idea.

'Thanks!'

His voice was gruff with gratitude, but Anna shrugged it off.

'Anyone would have done it—and as far as Penny's concerned, I think anyone would have done. She needed someone to listen to her, nothing more. Now, we really should get her to bed.'

'I suppose we should,' Tom agreed, but he didn't move, though the hand that had touched her hair earlier had found its way back there, and was now stroking her, as gently as he'd stroked Cass that first night at her house.

'I've got to go,' she whispered, forgetting she'd intended staying—forgetting everything except the effect that tender touch was having on her body.

'Are you sure of that?' Tom asked, as if he could read exactly how she felt in the texture of her hair.

'Yes, I'm sure,' she said, and turned to disentangle herself from Penny. But the movement brought her closer to Tom, and he had only to turn his head for their lips to meet.

This is wrong, wrong, wrong, her conscience shouted, but unless a lightning bolt came down from the sky and stopped them, she was going to let him kiss her—and probably kiss him back, though, given the way Penny was slumped against her, nothing else could possibly happen.

Then lights illuminated the steps again—not a lightning bolt but another car, presumably Carrie's, sweeping up the drive.

'Saved by the return of the sisterhood,' Tom said lightly, then he bent, and with only a slight grunt of effort lifted his sister into his arms.

That incident meant nothing to him, Anna thought as she walked out to her car. Or at least nothing more than a mild flirtation.

And as it couldn't mean anything more for her either, she couldn't understand why she was upset.

CHAPTER EIGHT

ANNA returned home, tired and dispirited, to find Cassie, perhaps able to smell smoke, prowling around the kitchen and twitching nervously. Picking up the cat, she walked through to her bedroom. Maybe they both needed company tonight.

Waking after a restless sleep, she found Cassie had deserted her, and though nothing more than the faintest smell of smoke lingered in the air, the cat still prowled and twitched, yowling now as she did her round of the kitchen.

'I guess it's better than having you sitting in your travelling cage, looking sulky,' Anna told the cat, although she did wonder if perhaps this behaviour was because she'd moved the cage from the kitchen, shutting it away in a storeroom at the back of the house.

Cassie didn't enlighten her, and though sorely tempted to call Tom and ask about this latest erratic cat behaviour, Anna knew it was the last thing she should do.

She had to see less of him, not more. And with the entire town in cahoots to see that *didn't* happen, she'd have to be extra vigilant about keeping her distance.

She had a quick breakfast, then, with no morning surgery, set off for town, grateful, given her working hours, that the supermarket opened on Sunday mornings. She'd do her shopping early, then spend the day at home, doing domesticated things like laundry and tidying the house. After which she'd write a long letter to her parents, telling them all about life in the outback and the new things she was learning. She'd write to Gay, her best friend from for ever as well, and maybe even Philip, though he never wrote back, preferring to phone.

With this satisfactory plan in mind, she smiled as she shopped, greeting people she passed in the aisles, stopping to listen to tales of the fire or how little Adam was getting over his chickenpox. The open, easy friendliness of the locals gave her a sense of belonging but she guessed they still held something back—that becoming one of them would take longer than the six months she had.

'Takes fifty years,' Barb at the checkout told her when Anna mentioned this, asking how long it took to be counted as a local. 'I've been here twenty-two years and they still think of me as a newcomer.'

Anna smiled, but deep inside she felt again that unexpected twinge of loneliness—the longing for a friend.

'At least I've got Cassie, even if she does prefer Tom to me,' she comforted herself as she drove home and unloaded plastic bags full of groceries from her car.

Struggling with the bags, she had to lean over and turn the back doorknob with her chin, then she kicked open the kitchen door and walked in, stumbling on something she must have dropped on the floor before she left.

Something soft?

She looked down, dropped the groceries and let out a desperate cry. The beautiful animal was dead. She knew it but couldn't help herself, scooping up the limp body and racing back out to the car.

Driving the way Tom had driven her to Dani's place, she screeched to a halt outside Tom's house only minutes later. Thank heavens his car was there—he was home.

He came hurrying out from behind the surgery, no doubt alerted to her arrival by the screech of brakes and splatter of gravel as she'd pulled up. Not in blue today, but in khaki overalls, unbuttoned from the waist up, long sleeves rolled to the elbow as his shirts always were, the long legs of the garment tucked into boots that finished just below his knees.

All this Anna took in as she lifted the cat out and raced towards him.

'It's Cassie,' she cried. 'I found her on the floor like this. Tell me she's not dead, Tom. Tell me she's not dead.'

Tom caught her in his arms and held her steady for a moment, then carefully eased away and lifted the cat from her trembling hands.

'You know she's dead, Anna,' he said quietly, 'but it was right to bring her here. We have to find out how she died.'

He walked towards the surgery, carrying the cat as gently as if she were still alive.

'But she was my friend,' Anna sobbed, aware she was losing it but unable to cope with all that was happening a minute longer.

Tom opened the door and led the way inside, through a tiled reception area, into what was clearly an operating theatre. Which, from the water splashed everywhere, he'd been hosing down when she'd arrived.

He put Cassie down on the table in the middle and turned on a bright operating light. Then he reached out and once again drew Anna close, tucking her up against his body so her tears splashed against his chest.

'I know,' he said gently, smoothing his hand down her hair. He let her cry for a few minutes but, comforting though it was to be held against him and interesting though the texture of his chest and swirl of chest hair was beneath her cheek, she knew this wasn't exactly avoidance. She straightened, muttering apologies for behaving so pathetically, then turned her attention to the cat.

'Could someone have poisoned her?' she asked. 'Could I have given her something inadvertently?'

Tom's eyes narrowed when she asked these questions and he nodded, as if acknowledging that she'd shifted emotionally as well as physically away from him.

'It's more likely snakebite. With the drought and the

dams drying up, snakes are coming closer to the houses in town in search of food—frogs.'

'But Cassie never goes outside,' Anna protested. 'She might have accepted the move to Merriwee to the extent she gave up the travelling cage, but nothing would tempt her out into what she must have considered wilderness.'

Tom said nothing. He was examining the cat, running his hands carefully over it, smoothing the hair backwards as if seeking something.

'There,' he said at last, pointing to the skin on her left cheek. 'See the puncture marks. Snake.'

'But she hasn't been outside,' Anna repeated. 'In fact, last night she was prowling around the kitchen and making such a fuss I thought she might want to go out. I opened the door and left it open but she wouldn't deign to look in that direction.'

'She was prowling and making a fuss?'

Anna nodded in answer to the repeated question. 'And yowling,' she added. 'Making a terrible noise.'

'Come on,' he said, turning to take her hand and lead her out of the theatre.

'Where are we going?' Anna demanded.

'Where am *I* going,' he said. 'You're staying right here. You can talk to Penny, you're good at that. You can even talk to Grace and Carrie if you like, but stay here until I get back.'

'Why? Where are you going?' Anna demanded, tugging her hand out of his and refusing to move another inch until she knew what was happening.

'To your place. That cat died of snakebite and if she hasn't been outside, it means the snake is inside. That's why she was upset.'

Anna felt as if all her blood was draining away and must have swayed, for Tom reached out and caught her.

'Don't you dare faint,' he said sternly. 'You're far too big to carry any distance. I might do it over a threshold one day, but any further than that would be asking too much of a man.'

She knew he was joking—about the threshold—to make her feel better, but, coming on top of the death of Cassie, it was too much. Stupid tears—for someone who never cried—slid down her cheeks so Tom had to hold her close again, and smooth her hair, and pat her back, murmuring, 'There, there,' in such a husky voice it didn't sound at all like him.

He held her for long enough for her to recover her composure—and perhaps a little longer—then ordered her up to the house.

'Pen's around somewhere, she'll make you a cup of tea.'

He touched her lightly on the cheek, then added, 'On second thoughts, you might be better making your own cup of tea. She's far too impatient to wait for the water to boil, and tea made with warm water just doesn't work.'

He was trying so hard to make her feel better that Anna forced her lips to smile. She knew it wasn't much of an effort but, as it turned out, she doubted Tom had noticed. He'd walked away, returning with a strange, long-handled object and a hessian bag.

'Snake-catcher,' he explained, fiddling a string to show how jaws at the end of the pole opened and closed.

'You don't need to catch the snake!' Anna was so appalled the words came out in a panic-induced screech. 'Just kill the bloody thing!'

'''Just kill the bloody thing''!' Tom mimicked her accent, then grinned. 'Tut-tut! What would your patients think to hear you swearing that way? You've been in the bush too long, Dr Talbot.'

But his smile and teasing only accelerated her panic.

'I'm serious, Tom. I don't know much about poisonous snakes but I know that trying to catch them is a great way to get bitten.'

'So is trying to kill them,' he said, more sober now.

'Interfering with them in any way is likely to frighten them into attacking, but it can't stay in your house for ever.'

'I don't mind. I could shift in here. You said yourself you've tons of room. And it's not far from the hospital.'

She knew she was being unreasonable, but fear for Tom had thrust common sense down to some subterranean level of her mind.

'Or I could get a flat in town.'

She was babbling now, and the suggestion was totally irrational, but every protective instinct in her body was protesting against his plan.

'Calm down!' He squeezed her shoulder. 'I've done this heaps of times before. I'll capture the snake, take it out into the bush and release it back where it belongs.'

The enormity of this new suggestion—which entailed driving some kilometres with a poisonous snake in the car—was so great, Anna couldn't speak at all. Well, not until she'd walked across to her car and opened the door.

'No you won't,' she said, sliding in behind the wheel. 'Because it's my house and I won't let you in. I'm going back to lock it up and I'll leave it locked up for ever.'

Tom's burst of laughter told her just how stupid that idea was, but it wasn't until he came c   t in and twitched the car keys from her finge   came really annoyed.

'Give them back,' she ordered, but he ignored her, merely touching her cheek once again, this time with a gentle forefinger.

'All in good time,' he promised softly. 'But in the meantime, you stay here.'

He walked away, then turned back. 'I won't do anything foolish,' he promised. 'I've far too much to live for to put my life at even the slightest risk.'

The words seemed heavy with multi-layered meanings but, far from reassuring Anna, they only deepened her apprehension. Her fear for him might have lessened—

slightly—but her reaction to his words—a bizarre kind of excitement—was frightening in a different way. Jolted and confused, she remained sitting where she was until long after he'd driven away.

'I saw you out there. Come in. I'll make you a cup of tea.'

Penny appeared at the window of Anna's car.

'Come on! I'm still a bit spotty but you already told me I'm not contagious,' she reminded Anna, opening the door and waiting impatiently for her to get out. 'I want to thank you for being kind to me last night. Fancy me losing it like that. And, actually, I've a lot of other things to tell you. While I was in bed with the spots, I read through the letters. You know, the ones Mum sent on to Tom. And I think I've found a woman who sounds just right. I want you to read it to see what you think.'

Bizarre didn't begin to cover Anna's reactions this time.

'You shouldn't read other people's mail,' she reminded Penny, speaking sharply enough for the young girl, who'd headed back towards the house, to pause and turn towards her.

'But Tom said I could.'

'Oh!'

Penny had moved on again, so Anna had to get out of the car and follow if she wanted to continue the conversation.

Which she did!

'But he didn't say I could,' she reminded Penny. 'Besides, do you really think you're qualified to choose a wife for your brother? And do you really think he wants one?'

'Of course he wants one.' Penny had swung around, and the determined look in her blue eyes, so like Tom's, confirmed her certainty. 'Milk in your tea?' she asked, as if tea had been the sole topic of conversation.

Anna nodded, remembering Tom's warning as she watched Penny pour the watery brew.

'You see, once he's got a wife, then we—my sister and I—won't have to worry about him ever again. We won't have to worry about him bringing someone who's likely to be a pain into the family, or about some woman taking him for a ride, or hurting him the way Grace did, though, actually, I don't think he was ever that much in love with her. It was just he thought she suited him and it was time he settled down.'

She'd skipped over *her* suitability—or not—as a matchmaker, and Anna decided not to go there again. She didn't know how long Tom would be and, though reading other people's mail was about as wrong as you could get, she couldn't help wanting to know more about this paragon Penny had chosen for her brother.

So she, Anna, could send poison-pen letters to her?

Or make a voodoo doll and stick pins in it?

Don't be ridiculous.

It's none of your business.

But the longer the silent argument went on, the weaker it became, so when Penny returned from a foray out of the kitchen, brandishing a letter in her left hand, Anna knew she'd lost.

'If you feel bad about reading it, I can read it out loud,' Penny offered, but, generous though the offer was, Anna didn't accept. She felt enough empathy with the unknown writer to not want Penny making mockery of the words.

'I'll read it myself, though I still think you should leave your brother to choose his own wife.'

'He goes on looks mostly, and convenience—someone who's around. I suppose, left to him, he'd choose you,' Penny said.

'I'm not available,' Anna snapped, and all but snatched the letter from Penny's fingers.

But far from being aggravated by her guest's behaviour, Penny actually smiled—a smile that left Anna feeling even more apprehensive than she had earlier.

Had Penny indeed found a paragon who would make Tom the perfect wife? Was that why she was smiling?

Anna opened the letter, though her fingers sensed her reluctance and fumbled with the sheets of paper.

The woman was indeed a paragon and beautiful as well, if the enclosed photograph was actually of her and not some movie star.

'See, she loves the country, grew up on a property, can fence and brand and muster and she's even won the sponge-cake competition at local shows. My mum says a sponge cake is the hardest thing to cook. She says they're not worth the bother, because they hardly ever turn out right.'

Anna frowned at her youthful informant.

'Why's it important Tom's wife can make a sponge cake?'

'Bake a sponge cake,' Penny corrected, then she added triumphantly, 'Because it's what country women do!'

'But they do more than that,' Anna protested. 'I've met many of them, talked with them. They teach their children, and they help their husbands on the farms, and they are on committees and do meals-on-wheels and run swimming clubs for the kids. They do more, probably, than city women, as they don't want their children missing out on opportunities they might have had in larger towns. I don't see where sponge cakes come into it.'

'It's a country thing,' Penny said, as if that was enough for her to win the argument.

Anna let it drop, though Penny's conversation had left her with a strange feeling of inadequacy.

As if you'd ever need to bake a sponge cake, her mental self chided, especially once you're married to Philip, who has chefs in every house and apartment he owns. But there was no escaping it—this woman, who, even discounting the sponge cake, could do so many things Anna couldn't do, would be perfect for Tom.

'Well, what do you think?' Penny demanded, but Anna couldn't force her lips to put her thoughts into words.

She merely nodded, and passed the letter back to Penny, then sipped at the now cold as well as tasteless tea. But the thought of Tom being matched up with the wonder-woman made it curdle in her stomach and, knowing she had to escape before she revealed her turmoil, she rinsed her cup and announced she should be off.

'I'd come with you, but I've got to draft a letter for Tom to send to Annabel.'

The suggestion was so outrageous Anna had to protest.

'*You're* going to draft the letter? Isn't that taking things a bit too far?'

'Not at all,' Penny said, waving the letter airily around between them. 'If I leave it to Tom, he could take ages and we really need to get Annabel up here. Mum and Patience will be up in the holidays soon and it would give them a chance to meet her—and her to meet them.'

Anna's thumb slid to press against her engagement ring.

'And my pretend engagement to Tom? How do you intend to handle that?'

'I don't!' Penny told her, grinning cheekily. 'That's up to you. Or Tom. One of you will have to break it off.'

She paused and frowned, then added, 'And you'd better do it soon, otherwise she'll get here, and someone will mention it, and she might think he's chosen her on the rebound.'

'Rather than have his sister pick her out of a hat!' Anna retorted, then she spun around and marched away. Penny could make what she wanted of the snappish reply!

But as she stormed away, she remembered what had brought her to the vet's this morning, and a sense of loss threatened to overwhelm her. She climbed back into her car and rested her head against the steering-wheel.

Poor Cassie, she thought, but then she realised some of the sorrow she felt was self-pity. She pulled herself together and finally remembered she didn't have keys. Anger at Tom dispelled some of the sadness, but then she began to worry about snakebite antivenin and wonder what the hospital had on hand.

Suppose he'd been bitten while she sat here feeling sorry for herself…

Nervous and fearful, she set off through the trees, sure she'd eventually find her way back to her house. The thought of snakes made her jumpy, so she skittered at every rustle of grass, finally reaching home, dishevelled and exhausted, though the exhaustion was more mental than physical.

There was no sign of Tom, but he'd left a note on the door.

'If you come back before I see you, you can go in. Have removed unwanted guest—a red-bellied black—poisonous enough to kill poor Cassie, but you'd probably have survived a bite.'

'No, I wouldn't,' Anna muttered, tearing the note from the door and crumpling it in her hand. 'I'd have died of fright!'

And though that might have been a slight exaggeration, it was one more reminder of just how inadequately qualified she was for life in the outback. Annabel would probably have killed the damn snake by biting off its head!

'You're not setting up for life in the outback,' Anna reminded herself, then had a further reminder of her future when she played back the messages on her answering-machine.

'Thought I'd drop in and see you next week, darling,' Philip's cheery voice announced. 'My pilot tells me the jet won't be able to land at your local strip, but there's a place called Three Gorges we can come into. He'll arrange on-ward transport from there and someone will let you know an ETA.'

'Oh, will someone?' Anna grumped, though the loneliness she had been feeling should have been relieved by this message, and her body should have been producing at least a modicum of excitement at the thought of Philip's visit.

But all she felt was a return of the apprehension that seemed to haunt her these days, and though she knew Philip would understand about the pretend engagement, she might have to rehearse just how to explain it to him.

'The only good thing is,' she said to the answering-machine, which was no more responsive than the cat had ever been, 'he's always so busy he won't stay long, so the locals won't even know he's here and I won't have to explain two fiancés.'

But this sensible deduction didn't restore her equilibrium and, as the house was too lonely without her feline friend, she walked over to the hospital, seeking refuge in her office and distraction in some paperwork.

Philip's arrival, five days later, caused the kind of stir Anna imagined was usually reserved for visiting royalty. For a start, one of his PR people had seen fit to inform the local newspaper of his arrival, so the midweek paper had a huge bold headline announcing SOUTH AFRICAN TYCOON'S VISIT, followed by speculation on whether he might be considering buying property in the area, or perhaps reopening the long-defunct copper mine.

'I heard it was to do with diamonds,' Barb at the supermarket confided to Anna when she was in buying some extra provisions for Philip's stay. 'That someone had found a diamond pipe—that's a funny thing to call it—nearby and this bloke's coming to stake a claim.'

Anna suppressed a smile at the thought of Philip physically staking anything. She also hoped he was travelling with his usual entourage, which would include a cook. His cooks invariably carried their own provisions with them, so it wouldn't matter that Anna couldn't get smoked salmon or Beluga caviar at Merriwee's only supermarket.

'That your bloke flying in?'

It was probably inevitable she'd bump into Tom as she walked out, while the thought of Philip as a 'bloke'—and he'd been twice described this way now—made her shake her head.

'It's not? I thought for sure it was! I mean, how many tycoons named Philip can there be in the world, especially ones with an interest in Merriwee?'

By now Anna was so confused—physically as well as mentally—she couldn't reply. Not that her lack of comment stopped Tom. In fact, he continued, as if afraid the silence might bite him if he let it lie between them.

'I guess from the look on your face it is him. Will it cause a problem? Do you want me to explain to him, man to man, about the engagement? I could take him up the pub for a beer.'

Another impossible image somersaulted through Anna's mind but, in fact, it was exactly what happened when Philip finally arrived, late on Friday afternoon. The helicopter bringing him and his party from Three Gorges was unable to land at the hospital because Anna was organising the emergency evacuation of a heart-attack victim.

'I've told him to come down over at Tom's place,' Jess reported to Anna, who was battling her own nerves *and* a serious drop in electrolytes in her patient's body. 'I've phoned Tom and warned him.'

'How come you've been talking to a helicopter pilot? And how do you know he can land at Tom's?' Anna took her attention away from the patient for long enough to question Jess's authority.

Jess grinned.

'The pilot's my husband and he's landed there before. He picked me up from there after work one day. You see, he's not supposed to land in the hospital grounds, though he has done it once or twice.'

Anna would have liked to have asked how Jess's husband came to be flying Philip into town, but it had all become too complicated, and her patient needed too much of her attention for her to be diverted into unimportant issues.

Though the nausea in her stomach suggested the meeting between Tom and Philip didn't quite fall into the 'unimportant issue' category.

Two hours later the helicopter she was waiting for finally arrived, but it was still another hour before she was satisfied her patient was stable enough to move.

Anna watched the bulky emergency aircraft lift off the ground, but felt no easing of the tension that had gathered in her shoulders during the long battle to save her patient's life. What she'd really like to do was go home, have a long soak in a hot bath, then go to bed, but, although it was now after nine, Philip would still be expecting her. Regular phone calls from the motel to the hospital had left her in no doubt about that!

Jess had passed on most of the messages, though Anna had got away long enough to speak to him herself.

'I've brought Carl with me—was he with me before you left? He's a chef who trained at a top restaurant in London. I found him at a fishing lodge in Scotland, would you believe?'

Anna did believe. It was the kind of thing Philip did, picking up people all over the world and adding them to his entourage. In a way, she realised, he'd done much the same with her.

And her parents…

And cousin Joe, Uncle Fred's son…

And her friend Gay…

They mightn't all travel with him, but they were members of what Philip considered his 'people', and, she had to admit, he took care of them well.

As the lights from the helicopter became fainter, she moved away, not returning to the hospital but heading to her little house. Another fiancé might have been waiting there—wanting to be alone with her when she finally finished work—but that wasn't Philip's way. He was a social animal, happiest in a crowd, surrounded by friends both old and new.

'He'll have all the guests at the motel and probably half the staff eating Carl's food by now,' she muttered to herself as she wearily stripped off her dirty clothes and stepped under the shower.

Then, in spite of the warmth of the water, she shivered, hoping Grace and Carrie were still at Tom's and not part of Philip's party. It was one thing to believe he'd understand the false engagement when she told him of it, but for him to hear it from someone else…

'It's OK, I explained about the engagement and he understands.'

Anna had pulled up outside the motel, surprised to find a space—there were so many cars parked there. Then, as Tom's voice came out of the darkness, she wondered if it had been coincidence.

'I heard the emergency chopper taking off and came out to shift my car so you could have my space and not have to walk too far. Half the town's come along to meet the great tycoon.'

She'd felt a little glow of pleasure when he'd explained about the parking space—it was such a Tom kind of thing for him to have done—but his presence was far from reassuring. In fact, his presence was causing such upheaval in her body she wanted to get back into her car and drive away.

Perhaps back to Melbourne!

'Anyway, as I said, when Philip arrived I took him and his crew up to the pub—old Mavis there was delighted to have so many extra drinkers. I got him on his own and explained the situation to him, man to man.'

Perth was further away than Melbourne—she'd drive to Perth!

'So, are you coming in?'

'Are you going back in there?' Anna asked, and, now her eyes had adjusted to the dimly lit footpath, saw him hesitate.

'I think he'll expect me to,' he said, his voice gruff with some emotion Anna couldn't understand. 'You see, he's told people you're a friend he's dropped in to see—he hasn't mentioned your engagement. He did it as a favour to me, Anna, nothing more, but if you go in and I don't, people might notice.'

'They wouldn't if I broke off this stupid engagement right now!' Anna snapped at him, knowing there was no way her nerves could stand the strain of being in the same room with both Tom and Philip.

'Or I could get a call. Yes, we'll do that. You can go in, say you met me coming out and I've had to go out of town to see a—a sick stud bull would be best. I don't do a lot of night calls so it has to be something important.'

'A sick stud bull,' Anna repeated, and, though she should have been glad Tom had thought of this excuse and wouldn't be there to witness her meeting with Philip, she was far from easy over telling more outright lies than had already been propagated. 'This is ridiculous!'

'Yes, isn't it?' Tom said, then he reached out and drew her close, pressing her body hard against his. For a moment Anna assumed it was simply more of Tom's tactile stuff, but then he kissed her, burning her lips with a passion she'd never felt before but which her body recognised and returned a hundredfold.

Some tiny cell in her brain registered that there were

worse things than being in the same room with Tom and Philip, but the rest of her brain—and all her body—was enjoying the kiss too much to let the killjoy cell ruin the moment.

Then, what could have been a minute or an aeon later, Tom's hands shifted to her shoulders, and he eased their bodies apart.

'Goodbye,' he said, running his forefinger down the line of her cheek, and tracing her jaw bone. 'Goodbye, my beautiful Anna.'

The huskiness in his voice told her he meant it, and her heart grew heavy in her chest.

But why would Tom be saying goodbye?

Had Philip said something to him?

Or maybe Tom was going to get into his car and drive away. Maybe he was driving to Perth…

Telling herself she wouldn't get any answers from watching his car drive off, Anna walked into the motel, past the deserted reception desk, following the sound of voices and laughter.

'Darling girl, how are you? Exhausted, I bet! Come here and sit down. I've got champagne chilled to exactly the right temperature and a glass is what you need to perk you up.'

Philip's lips met her cheek with a chaste kiss, and with his arm protectively around her shoulders he led her into the mêlée. There must have been thirty or forty people crammed into the motel's small dining room, most of the faces familiar though Anna couldn't put names to more than a dozen.

A dozen that included Grace and Carrie.

As if feeling her tension, Philip gave her a reassuring squeeze.

'I won't say a word,' he whispered, and Anna realised he was enjoying both the sensation his arrival in town had caused and the role Tom had persuaded him to play.

'Actually,' he whispered, 'I was relieved to meet your vet. It was the photo of the two of you, sent on to me by my clipping service, that prompted me to come.'

'A photo sent on by your clipping service?' Anna was so stunned her voice had risen to a shrill squeak.

'Hush, I'll explain later,' Philip said, waving his free hand towards a waiter who was hovering with a napkin-wrapped bottle of champagne. 'Have a drink.'

Anna spun away from him, so she could look him in the face.

'I don't want a drink, Philip,' she said crisply. 'I'm already tired and I'm still on call, so a drink isn't a good idea. But I do want an explanation. I want to know why you have a clipping service keeping tabs on me.'

One thing that could be said for Philip, Anna acknowledged as he excused the two of them, explaining he had messages and gifts from Anna's family to pass on. He could get himself smoothly out of just about any situation.

Having exhorted those present to keep partying, he ushered her out of the room, past the reception desk and down another corridor to his room.

Once inside, he closed the door, leaned back on it and took her in his arms, touching her hair, her cheek, her neck.

'Oh, my beautiful Anna,' he murmured, unknowingly echoing words she'd already heard this evening. 'It is *so* good to see you. And so thoughtless of me to let you walk into that rowdy party when we needed time alone.'

He smiled then kissed her on the lips.

'Hello, my darling.'

And though the kiss was nice enough, his apology genuinely contrite, she still couldn't relax.

Or forget the clipping service…

'A kiss won't make things better this time, Philip,' she told him, and felt him stiffen.

She was startled by his reaction, then wondered if this was the first time she'd ever not allowed herself to be sweet-talked out of anger with him. She'd been angry but had given in when he'd whisked her parents away from their suburban home and installed them in a small mansion in the grounds of his estate. Though later she'd cooled down because she'd imagined they were delighted with their change in circumstances...

She brushed away the memories. The issue here was the clipping service.

'I can't believe you've got people searching out mentions of my name—sending you reports on my behaviour.'

'It was an accident, sweet thing,' he said, moving away from her and opening the small refrigerator, which, one glance showed, had been stocked by him or his staff, not the motel. 'Sit down. You mightn't be able to have a drink, but I could do with one. I've been very abstemious in there, knowing you'd eventually arrive. I think I deserve one now.'

She watched him, seeing him with a stranger's eyes, listening with a stranger's ears, and wondering if she really knew this man.

'The clipping service clips all kinds of things for me, mainly business information, but information on my competitors as well. When you won the scholarship to university, I asked them to clip items with your name in as well—you know, results, and honours awarded, that kind of thing.'

Thank heaven I was never arrested in a student protest or for being drunk and disorderly, Anna thought, then Philip was talking again.

'I just forgot to tell them to stop clipping,' he said, beaming at her and raising his glass towards her. 'So, when they sent me a photo of you and some stranger, with a heading AUSTRALIA'S LAST ELIGIBLE BACHELOR MEETS HIS MATCH, naturally I was curious.'

'The magazine printed that?' Anna demanded, as new anger, directed elsewhere this time, fired along her nerves.

'That double-crossing Carrie! She promised Tom she wouldn't, in exchange for getting exclusive rights to the wedding photos.'

'The wedding photos?' Philip repeated, subsiding into a chair. 'I thought this engagement was pretence.'

Anna gave an exasperated shrug.

'Of course it is and the wedding is as well. Tom made it up to stop both Carrie and Grace going on about the engagement. As she's at your party, you've probably met Grace—well, Tom made it up because she was suspicious.'

The whole thing sounded unbelievable even to her own ears so she had no idea how it sounded to Philip, but that wasn't the point, she remembered.

The point was the clipping service.

'I still don't like the feeling you've been spying on me,' Anna told him, then realised she might have pushed too far as Philip's eyes narrowed and he studied her in a cold manner she'd seen before but had never had directed her way.

Then he smiled and she wondered if she'd imagined it.

'I can understand that,' he said, 'but be reasonable, pet. Do you think I like this pretence you've perpetrated here? Do you think it suited me to come thousands of miles out of my way to find out what was going on? I know I said I'd give you six months to get this outback nonsense out of your system, but I was never happy about it. Come back with me now. Come back home. Apparently you've become quite adept at making up stories, so you'll think of something. Sick family member. Homesickness. Something.'

Anna stared at him, unable to believe what was happening. He was smiling as he spoke of her making up stories—sharing a joke—but underneath his soft tone there was an edge of steel. Almost as if he was ordering her home—as if she were an employee, not a cherished fiancée.

Sheer disbelief made speech impossible, then panic set in as she realised just how entangled her life and that of her family had become with Philip's.

Fighting the drowning sensation this realisation caused, she sought not for a solution—clear thinking was impossible right now—but for a compromise.

'I can't just walk out and leave the hospital without a doctor,' she said, hoping a calm, quiet voice might impress the seriousness of the situation on him. 'I could give notice, but it would have to be a month. They wouldn't find even a locum in less time than that.'

Philip studied her for a moment.

'Then you'd come?'

For a moment Anna hesitated, weighed down with doubt and regret, then she thought of her parents—of her responsibility to them, and the gratitude she felt for all they'd given her.

They were settled in their home on Philip's estate…

'If I can get a replacement, I'll come,' she said.

Philip stood up and came towards her, smiling now— the genial, loving Philip she knew—but even as he reached out to take her in his arms there was a knock on the door and Carrie, accompanied by Bob Filmer, practically tumbled into the room.

'Come on, Phil,' she said. 'We're all starving and your chef fellow says if he has to hold the meal back any longer it will be ruined.'

Phil? Anna glanced at him but he seemed unperturbed by this casual, very Australian shortening of his name. She waited for him to tell them to go ahead without him— surely he'd want to be alone with her—but once again she was surprised. He nodded his agreement, then confirmed it with a cheery, 'We're on our way!' He turned to take Anna's arm.

But she was already fishing her pager out of her pocket.

'Sorry, I've got to go back to the hospital.' She waved

the pager in the air and kissed Philip on the cheek. 'Call me in the morning?'

He was angry again but that couldn't be helped. And he'd be even angrier if he guessed she'd told a lie—another lie! But there was no way she could have walked into that scene of jollity and pretended to enjoy herself, not with tension twisting her stomach into knots and uneasiness over Philip's behaviour burning along her nerves.

She might agree to his request that she return home, but nothing he could do or say would persuade her to attend his party.

Not that he argued.

In fact, he gave in quite gracefully—for Philip.

'Poor you!' he murmured, kissing her cheek once again. But his fingers tightened on her upper arm as if reminding her of her promise—or of her place in his life.

Something between an employee and a possession, she thought with sudden clarity. She should ask him if that's how he saw her, but Carrie was urging him away and it was Bob, admittedly at Philip's suggestion, who walked Anna to her car.

As she pulled up outside the hospital—so there hadn't been a page but at least she had told the truth when she'd said she was coming here—she looked at the dark patch of trees she knew shadowed Tom's house and smiled wryly to herself.

He on his own over there, she on her own here—practically the only people she knew in town who *weren't* enjoying Philip's hospitality.

CHAPTER NINE

PHILIP arrived at six the next morning, radiating love and goodwill.

'I phoned the hospital and the nurse on duty told me you'd got away by eleven so I knew I wouldn't be waking you after only a couple of hours' sleep.'

Anna, pyjama-clad and bleary-eyed, nodded at this information. She was standing in the doorway of her little house while Philip stood on the doorstep, the local taxi waiting, doors open, on the drive behind him.

'I brought breakfast,' he added, and smiled at her. 'Now, will you invite me in?'

'Invite you in?' Anna pushed her fingers through her straggly hair. She might have left the hospital at eleven, but having two fiancés hadn't promoted sound sleep. 'Of course.'

She stepped backwards, but Philip didn't follow, turning instead back towards the taxi.

There was a rumble of conversation, then doors slammed, an engine started up and Philip returned with a huge picnic basket.

'Carl tells me most things we like are unavailable in your outback town. He got the supermarket manager out of bed last night when I mentioned the picnic, but still couldn't do much.'

Anna watched in bemusement as Philip placed the basket on her dining table and began unloading packages, unwrapping things to reveal an array of tempting goodies.

'Blueberry muffins, mini smoked salmon quiches—he had a supply of smoked salmon with him—bacon-wrapped sausages, oven-baked tomatoes...'

A sense of unreality settled over Anna as Philip continued to display the goodies his chef had produced for their breakfast.

Was Philip always like this? Yes, food was important to him, and he took great delight in being able to provide delicacies for his friends and important guests.

But it was strange behaviour at six in the morning, visiting a fiancée he hadn't seen—apart from a brief interlude last night—for over a month.

Did he regret the way he'd spoken to her last night? All but ordering her to return home? Was this his way of apologising?

Anna realised she had no idea of the answers to her unspoken questions, and that realisation brought another question in its train.

How well did she know Philip?

'I'll have a quick shower and join you in a few minutes,' she told him, anxious to get away while she considered an answer.

Anxious to test him as well?

She wasn't sure if, subconsciously, she'd been doing that, but if she had, it didn't work. He didn't try to stop her. Didn't suggest he wash her back. Didn't make any move to hold or kiss or caress her...

New, unanswerable questions writhed uncomfortably in Anna's head as she showered then pulled on a skirt and top, dressing for work, not Philip.

The aroma of newly brewed coffee hit her as she left the bathroom, and she smiled at the man who was carefully pushing down the plunger of a small coffee-maker.

'Making your own coffee, Philip?' she teased, feeling at ease with him for the first time since his arrival.

He looked up and smiled.

'I've always told you I'm more domesticated than you realise. I can make a pot of tea as well. Dulcie taught me that!'

'How is Dulcie?' Anna asked, smiling herself as she thought of the kindly housekeeper who'd been Philip's nurse when he'd been a child.

'She's great. She sends her love.' He brought the coffee-pot across to the table, then corrected himself. 'Or she would have done if she'd known I was coming here.'

He held a chair for Anna and as she sat down, he bent and kissed her on the back of her neck. It was a caress, but that of a friend rather than a lover, and with a sense of sadness more than jealousy she wondered if he had a mistress travelling with him at the moment.

'Now eat,' he ordered, waving his hand across the spread. 'Did I tell you about the South American deal? I phoned you from there, didn't I? Well…'

He talked, his hands waving as he described places he'd seen, plants he would build, factories he hoped to buy. This was the Philip she knew, burning with enthusiasm for his latest project, wanting to share the challenges he so enjoyed with her.

He'd explained the way his mind worked to her once, years ago. Apparently, it was faster than most people's so he grasped concepts more quickly and could turn them into something concrete and so expand his empire. He'd explained also about the women he knew around the world—women he knew intimately but who meant nothing to him. No, he'd chosen Anna quite early—well before she had been aware he had had any interest in her. In fact, it hadn't been long after she'd won his firm's scholarship to university, and he'd presented her with the first of the cheques which would finance her studies, that he'd decided she would, one day, make an ideal wife.

She remembered him telling her this as he talked, and realised why she'd been included in the clipping service's list way back then. If she'd been arrested at a protest, or for any other reason, would he have turned his attention to another candidate for the elevated position of his wife?

'I don't know about leaving in a month, Philip,' she said, as all these things collided in her head just as he paused to try one of the mini-quiches. 'This is something I've wanted for so long, and I've barely found my feet here yet. To leave so soon…'

She let the sentence die, but watched for his reaction. A slight frown, quickly smoothed away.

'We won't spoil breakfast by talking about it now.' He smiled reassuringly, but Anna was far from reassured. While not exactly spoilt, Philip was used to getting his own way. Money made it easy, in both business and in his private life. After all, how many people would refuse to sell a polo pony, for instance, when the offer made was for twice or even three times its value?

'Did I tell you about the serviced apartment I looked at in Paris? I thought it would be ideal place for our honeymoon. It's close to the office, and…'

Anna surveyed the array of food and chose a tiny croissant, still warm. Had Carl had been up all night, preparing then cooking this treat? She broke it in half and buttered it, then ate it, sipping at her coffee, listening to Philip yet aware of other voices in her head.

Voices asking questions about her relationship with this man. Voices wondering how well she knew him. If she knew him at all.

The sudden jangling summons of the phone startled her, but she reached out automatically, lifting the receiver, giving her name.

'It's Jillian, Anna. We've just had a phone call from Jenny White. Her eighteen-month-old is convulsing.'

'Temperature?' Anna asked.

'She didn't know but said he felt hot. I told her to strip him off and use damp cloths to cool him down on the way in. The Whites are on a property about thirty kilometres out of town, so she'll be here in twenty minutes or so.'

'I'll be there,' Anna promised, checking her watch as she hung up.

She turned to Philip.

'That was an emergency call. I've got twenty minutes before the patient arrives. When do you have to leave?'

He gave her a funny little smile.

'Straight after breakfast. I've a meeting in Japan tomorrow morning and some people I have to see first. This wasn't a good idea, was it?'

Anna lifted her shoulders in an uneasy shrug.

'It could have been better,' she agreed, as guilt that things had gone so wrong gnawed away at her. 'Most times I could have arranged for the local doctor to cover my calls—even taken a day off—but Peter's away on a course this week. I'm sorry, Philip.'

He reached out and took her hand.

'No, my dear, I'm sorry. I should have trusted you— asked you about the photo over the phone—not come haring over here like some jealous maniac.'

He shrugged now, then added, 'After all, you know I have my occasional diversions, so I could hardly complain if you did likewise.'

The remark was so startling—and so unlike the Philip she thought she knew—Anna found herself gaping at him.

'You mean you wouldn't mind if I had an affair with someone else? Is that what you're saying? What about fidelity? About love? In fact, now you've brought it up, knowing about your diversions, as you call them, is one thing, but between accepting them and being happy about them there's a gap as wide as the Indian Ocean. I haven't made a fuss before because I assumed it would all stop once we were married, and until then, as I wasn't free to travel with you, I'd just have to ignore them.'

She glared at him across the table, but couldn't have put enough effort into it as he smiled and said, 'You're beautiful when you're angry.'

The remark made her even angrier, but it also made her wonder if he'd heard a word she'd said—if he *ever* listened to her.

'You've got to go soon,' he reminded her. 'And you haven't eaten enough to keep a mouse alive, so stop being angry—it gives you indigestion, eating when you're cross—and have a muffin or, look, there are friands as well. I told Carl how much you loved them.'

Anna looked at the plate he proffered and knew she'd choke on even the smallest bite of the tasty little almond cake. She shook her head, finished her coffee, then stood up.

'I'll talk to you soon,' she said, bending down to kiss Philip's cheek, then moving away before he could grasp her arm and foil her escape.

But as she crossed to the hospital, the hopelessness of her situation all but swamped her. Her life was so tangled up in Philip's, there was no way she could back out of the engagement now. She thought of Tom—of the way he'd held her last night—of the kiss—of the way he'd said goodbye.

Anna frowned at the memory.

Why goodbye?

She wasn't going anywhere…

Not yet.

CHAPTER TEN

WILLIAM WHITE was definitely feverish, though not convulsing when he reached the hospital.

'It frightened me to see him like that,' Jenny said, settling the infant onto the mattress of a cot prepared to receive him. 'Does it mean he's epileptic?'

'Probably not,' Anna assured her, turning as a rangy-looking man came into the room.

'I'm Bill White, William's dad,' he said, holding out his hand to Anna. 'Had to park the car.'

Anna nodded, then continued her examination of the now sleepy child.

'Febrile convulsions, caused by a high temperature, are not uncommon in infants and small children. I'd say that's all it was.'

She turned William's head and felt the heat in the auricle, the outer shell of his left ear.

'I'll have a look, but the redness suggests an ear infection. They can flare up suddenly and cause high temperatures.'

Both parents looked relieved to think it might be something so simple.

'I kept thinking meningitis,' Jenny said. 'My mother had a sister who died of meningitis when she was a baby. I was terrified.'

Anna understood, and when examination of little William's ear showed a prurient infection, she was able to confirm her diagnosis and assure the couple it would soon clear up with antibiotics.

'But I'd like to keep him here until his temperature stabilises,' she said, getting Jenny to hold the toddler while she injected penicillin into his arm. 'Would one of you be able to stay?'

'We'll both stay,' Bill said firmly, lifting the distressed little boy into his arms and rocking him back and forth. 'I don't want Jenny here worrying on her own.'

Anna beamed at them.

'I'm so glad to hear that,' she said, 'because there's this wonderful room in the hospital which I haven't been able to use yet. It has a double bed and, though I mightn't have to keep William overnight, you can both rest on it during the day.'

'A double bed?' Both the Whites looked stunned, but it was Jenny who questioned the statement.

Anna laughed.

'I know—that's exactly my reaction when I first arrived and saw this wonderful room, complete with double bed. But when I asked about it, and one of the nurses explained it was for couples who had an infant who needed hospitalisation, or maybe for a couple where one partner was undergoing treatment and the other wanted to be with him or her, I realised what a wonderful idea it was. Now I've a chance to admit someone into the room. My guess is the nurses on duty have already put a cot in there. They'll be expecting you to stay.'

The nurse who'd been assisting her nodded.

'That's right,' she said. 'We're the only hospital in the whole district that has the double room, and we're very proud of it. Come on, I'll take you there.'

She led the Whites away, leaving Anna free. She should pop back to her house and see if Philip was still there, but she was so confused over the things that had happened in the last twenty-four hours she didn't think she could handle any more revelations.

Or confusion!

She did a round instead, checking on all her patients,

smiling as she passed the double room and saw Bill bouncing experimentally on the double bed.

'It's your pretty face keeping me alive,' Mr Jenks told her when she arrived by his bedside.

'And here I thought it was my good doctoring,' she joked, but she knew the man was failing, the poisons his kidneys no longer removed from his body slowly affecting his whole system. 'You're not using the oxygen?'

He was sitting up and breathing with difficulty.

'I use it when I have to,' he told her. 'But having those tubes up me nose—makes me wonder what my old horse must have felt, with a metal bit shoved into his mouth all the time. Makes me real sorry for the old fellow, it does.'

Anna smiled at the analogy, but it made her wonder how a man who'd once taken mobs of cattle across thousands of miles of desert, felt when he was virtually tethered to a bed.

'Most of the old-timers who've lived rough out here in the bush accept death more easily than townsfolk,' Jess told her a little later, when they met in the kitchen for a quick coffee-break. 'I think because they lost mates in places where there was no help. And no one to sanitise death—no funeral director to whisk the remains away. All they could do was dig a grave and bury the body—mark it with a cross they'd make from stones or branches. No one has any idea how many unmarked graves are scattered across the outback.'

Anna nodded, seeing in her imagination the dust kicked up by moving cattle, the drover thrown from a horse or gored by an errant bull—even bitten by a snake—dying in his mate's arms. It was sobering, yet special in so many ways, not least because it gave her another glimpse into the heart of this place they called the outback.

She walked across to the surgery to tackle the morning's patients, and was pleased when, for once, there were no interruptions. A sleepless night and Philip's early arrival had left her feeling washed out, and, with the last patient seen, she headed home, pleased it was Saturday and there was no afternoon surgery. She'd have lunch, then a sleep…

A doomed idea, she realised as she approached the house and saw she had another visitor. Penny was sitting at her front door.

'I thought you should be home soon,' she announced cheerfully. 'Did you know your boyfriend took both Grace and Carrie when he left? They wouldn't all fit in the helicopter so some of his friends drove to Three Gorges. Carrie's going to travel with him and do a story on the life of a jet-setting tycoon. She says it's far more interesting than outback bachelors. And he's offered Grace a job in one of his overseas companies. She says a top executive position is what she's always wanted, which made Tom mad as a hornet because he realised her excuse of not being able to live in the country on account of her allergies wasn't true.'

Anna found she wasn't altogether surprised about the first of these revelations. Philip tended to pick up people wherever he went.

Though in this case she sensed he may have had an ulterior motive. With the two women gone, Tom would no longer need a fiancée. And having met so many of the locals, Philip would have no difficulty contacting someone to check on the status of the 'engagement'.

A shiver of unease raced up Anna's spine—it was like the clipping service.

She really had to think about her relationship with Philip.

But whatever happened between her and Philip, she should break off the other engagement for Tom's sake.

Unless? foolish hope whispered.

There *is* no *unless*, she told it.

'Come in,' she said to Penny, then, finding Philip had

left the remaining food in the refrigerator, she invited her to share it for lunch.

'Will Tom be home this evening?' she asked, when the meal was done and Penny had declared her intention of walking uptown.

'Actually, he will. I know he's often out on Saturday nights, but I checked before I wrote to Annabel and I think he said he'd be home. I had to tell her what days were best for her to phone.'

Anna found herself contemplating strangling a complete stranger with a phone cord and decided she must be even more tired—if that was possible—than she'd thought.

'Well, I wouldn't want to interrupt an important phone call, but I need to see him. We have to break off this stupid engagement. Would you tell him I'll call over at about seven-thirty?'

Maybe her murderous tendencies would abate once she'd spoken to Tom.

Maybe!

Though even thinking about speaking to Tom made her heart race.

But it was impossible. Even if she *was* free, which she wasn't, she'd be all wrong for an outback wife. For a start, there was the sponge cake…

'You'll tell Tom?' she said, suspecting it was more for the pleasure of saying his name than pressing home the message.

Penny nodded. She was picking gravel out of the ripples in the sole of her sneaker and Anna wondered if she'd even heard, but she repeated the time and added, 'I'll tell him,' leaving Anna to assume the teenager would remember.

Penny not only remembered but she'd made herself scarce.

'She's gone to Mainyard with Jim and the horses,' Tom explained, coming down from the veranda as Anna got out of her car. 'The Boltons, who own the property, have offered to have her for a few nights, so I've gone from having a houseful of women to being on my own again.'

'Isn't that what you wanted? Isn't that good?' Anna asked, trying to still the stupid hammering of her heart against her ribs—telling herself she couldn't be nervous about breaking off a pretend engagement.

'I suppose so,' Tom said, obviously more concerned over his reply than her presence at his house because he'd already signed her out of his life with the goodbye he'd said the previous evening. 'Though I've got used to Penny being here. It's such a big house. When I first saw it, I imagined it full of Grace's and my children—I was an only child for long enough to realise a big family can be fun.'

He looked around, waited for her to mount the steps to the veranda, then added as he followed, 'I guess if I want to fulfil that dream, I'll have to get started soon.'

Anna's heart stopped its frantic beating and crunched itself into a small, hard ball in her chest. He was thinking of Annabel—waiting in for her to phone him.

Which meant Anna should say what she'd come to say and go—preferably somewhere far away. The word 'Perth' fluttered again in her head, though she knew putting a great physical distance between herself and Tom at the moment was impossible. She squared her shoulders, tilted her chin and wondered how to begin.

But he was talking again—about children and the Fleming genes being strong, as both his sisters had the same black hair and blue eyes as he did.

An image of a chubby three-month-old baby with a cap of shiny black hair and huge blue eyes appeared obligingly in Anna's head, making her wince with pain as she considered this child belonging to someone else. Somewhere along the line, she'd acknowledged she might actually love Tom Fleming, but nothing had prepared her for this agony!

'I'd like to have them while I'm still young enough to

play with them and enjoy them,' Tom was saying when Anna calmed down enough to catch the conversation. 'The children, I mean,' he added, as if she might have missed the bit that was upsetting her so much.

Anna took a deep breath, which didn't do much more than hurt her chest even more, then she took another, told herself she was a professional, trained to act as if calm and composed in the most horrendous situation.

'I guess you should be getting on with it, then.' She faltered over the words, trying to sound offhand and casual, while only too aware she didn't want him having children with Annabel. If you came right down to it, the fact of the matter was she didn't want him having children with anyone but herself. Hence the pain she was feeling.

The thought was so startling it affected her breathing, so the words, 'Have you someone in mind?' came out like a hoarse whisper.

He walked to the edge of the veranda and kicked a fallen blossom out into the darkness.

'Not really. Though Penny's found someone—one of the women who wrote to me. Pen keeps telling me she's perfect.'

If I don't strangle her first...

But if Tom met the paragon, he'd fall in love with her for sure—or at least like her too much to say no if she proposed to him, which was on the cards with Penny masterminding things.

Which would be good for Tom, surely?

A great wail of denial welled up inside Anna's head while desperation hammered in her heart. Without conscious consideration, she put her hands behind her back and wrenched off her engagement ring, shoving it deep into the back pocket of her denim skirt.

She took yet another deep breath, although she knew damn well they weren't helping, then stepped towards

Tom and held out her shaking but unadorned hands, palms downward so he couldn't help but see their ringless state.

'I'm not perfect, like Penny's paragon. In fact, I know I wouldn't be up to scratch as an outback wife. I can't fence and I'm a bit squeamish about branding, but as an only child I always wanted a big family, so I'd fit that part of your requirements.' She paused because she knew it was coming out all wrong—far too much information—but now she'd started, she knew she had to finish, even if it meant Tom thinking her an utter fool. She blurted out the final offer. 'What I'm saying is, I'm available if you want me.'

The silence was so complete Anna wondered if perhaps the world had ended, then an owl hooted in the distance, and closer to the house a frog began its croaky song.

'If I want you?' Tom said, his voice as croaky as the frog's.

He took her hands, squeezed her fingers tightly in his grasp, then leant forward and kissed her on the cheek, his lips lingering long enough for her to register the earthy scent of him.

'No,' he said, straightening up but retaining his grip on her hands.

'No?' Anna echoed, more in puzzlement than disbelief. Then disbelief kicked in. 'You *don't* want me?'

He sighed.

'Of course I want you. You're beautiful, kind, caring and totally wonderful. But no to your offer, Anna.' He gave a huff of totally humourless laughter. 'What a time to learn to say no to a woman, eh?' he added, dropping her hands to turn away from her, then leaning against the railing and looking out towards the shadowed fields beyond his garden.

'It's impossible, Anna. Perhaps if I'd never met your Philip… But I did. I talked to him. I even, against all odds, quite liked him. I knew then he was right for you. I said goodbye if you remember.'

Anna did remember, but before she could puzzle out the rest of what Tom had said he was speaking again.

'You'd said yourself it was an engagement you couldn't break, and, talking to him, I understood. I know he'd not only look after you, but your family as well. He can offer security to all the people you love. He can give you the world and probably the moon and stars as well, should you ask for them, which is no more than you deserve.'

Anna knew this was a kind of compliment, but she wasn't looking for compliments. She was looking for commitment and Tom was saying no...

'You have a couple of beers in the pub with this man, and suddenly you're the expert on my future,' she raged, crossing the veranda to stand behind him and glare ineffectually at his strong, broad back. 'What do you know anyway?' she continued, clasping her hands together so they didn't reach out to touch him. 'You're hardly living proof of a successful relationship!'

Tom turned and took her hands again, easing the tightness out of them with a gentle caress of his thumb across the backs of her fingers.

'I know you belong in Philip's world, not out here in the bush,' he said quietly, ignoring her jibe about relationships. 'I can picture you in an apartment in Paris, jetsetting from there to a ski-lodge in Arizona. Out here, you're like an orchid in a turnip field. At the moment, it's all new and different, and you're excited by the outback, but for ever? The romance of the bush can soon fade, Anna, when the heat and dust of a prolonged drought squeezes the colour from the landscape and hope from even the most optimistic of farmers. And when times are tough, it affects the town, not only financially—who's going to call in the vet, or buy a new car when the cattle are dying of hunger—but emotionally as well. Everyone suffers.'

Anna heard the sadness in his voice, but the anger still burning in her wouldn't allow her to acknowledge he might be feeling pain.

'You might as well add that I can't cook—no, bake's the right word—a sponge cake,' she muttered, wrenching her hands away from his and walking back towards the steps. 'Add that to the litany of reasons why I wouldn't make you a suitable wife!'

Tom watched her go, wondering, as she slammed the car door, if he should stop her driving when she was so uptight.

But it wasn't far back to the hospital and there was virtually no traffic on the roads at night.

He stayed on the veranda until he could no longer see the glow of her taillights, then, with a sigh, he turned and went back inside the big—and lonely—house. He was sure that, for probably the first time where a woman was concerned, he'd made the right decision.

So why was he feeling as if he'd been flattened by the council grader?

And where the hell did sponge cakes fit into the conversation?

Anna worked through the next few weeks in a cloud of misery which lifted only slightly when she forced herself to explore her surroundings. She camped out at the dam one night, and was rewarded by the sight of five kangaroos coming down to the water as dawn spread a soft pink glow across the sky. Sitting motionless in her sleeping bag, she saw the finely moulded heads with their huge brown eyes turn enquiringly towards her, then, perhaps sensing she meant them no harm, the family bent to drink.

She learnt, from Mr Jenks, that the little brown bird with the pink bonnet on the back of his head was a bower-bird, and the straggly arrangement of twigs he'd made under a shrub in her back yard was his bower, built and decorated with shiny white bones and glass to entice a female into mating with him.

Good luck to him!

The town, no doubt after her first ringless foray to the supermarket, seemed to know she was no longer engaged to Tom, so on the rare occasions she managed to make it to a social event she wasn't expected to spend time with him. Though seeing him, and not spending time with him, made the occasions so agonising she began to avoid parties where he might be present.

This restricted her to morning tea at the kindergarten where she talked about germs and hand-washing, and lunch with the senior citizens where she presented awards for community service.

'So much excitement might be bad for me,' she said wryly to Philip, who still phoned regularly, the first time to protest over her returning his ring, but more recently, she felt, because he was in the habit of talking to her. Her father, he'd assured her, was a valued employee and her parents could remain on in their house for as long as they wished, even after her father retired.

This comforted Anna, but apparently didn't please her mother, who forthrightly said she'd be glad to get away from Philip's stifling influence. 'In fact,' she told Anna, not long after the engagement was broken off, 'now we're not going to be related, your father can take early retirement. We're far too young to be cooped up on Philip's estate. We want to see the world and we might as well start with Australia.'

So they'd be coming while Anna was still at Merriwee, and would arrive in time to spend Christmas with her. But though she longed for their company, and the security of their unconditional love, it didn't fill the empty, aching place in her heart.

The place where Tom should be...

CHAPTER ELEVEN

THEN Bertha Spragg was admitted to the hospital with a badly ulcerated leg.

A big-boned, cheerful, youthful eighty-eight, Bertha must have been 'auntie' to half the town, so many visitors gathered in her room, bringing flowers, fruit, chocolates and gossip.

Plenty of gossip!

Anna learnt that Tom's stepmother and his other sister had arrived to stay, which might have explained why she herself hadn't seen anything of Penny lately, though for the week after that final goodbye to Tom—or, to put it correctly, Tom's final goodbye to her—Penny had continued to pop in, full of news of Annabel whose list of virtues had grown daily.

Anna also learnt that Bertha had, for close on sixty years, been the best sponge-cake maker not only in Merriwee but in the entire district. Using her parents' arrival as an excuse—though she suspected it was prompted by a mix of her niggly jealousy of Annabel and the need to find something to do with her spare time—Anna asked Bertha for a recipe.

'I'll actually need more than a recipe,' she told her bedridden patient. 'I'll need any tip you can give me, and possibly a couple of minor miracles. I can cook to feed myself, and once, when I was at school, I made a batch of biscuits, but the oven to me is just the bit of the stove that brings my hot-plates up to bench level.'

Bertha assured her that, under her tutelage, even if it was from a hospital bed, Anna would soon become an expert.

So, the great sponge-cake baking exercise began, consuming more and more of free Anna's time—and more eggs, sugar and flour than she wanted to think about—as she strove to produce a perfect cake.

'Forget perfect!' she muttered to herself, scowling at her latest effort which resembled nothing more than a lopsided-looking frisbee. 'Edible would do!'

Frustration needed an outlet and she was hurling this burnt offering across her back yard when Tom's big four-wheel-drive came around the corner of the hospital and pulled up outside her house.

'What's that you're throwing?' he asked, climbing down and peering suspiciously at her.

'A sponge cake,' Anna snapped, furious at her reaction to seeing him, and with him for causing it.

'A sponge cake?' he echoed in total disbelief, then he shook his head as if to clear it of such extraneous information and added, 'Not that it matters. I didn't come to talk to you about sponge cakes—'

He broke off and peered uncertainly towards the final resting place of the failure.

'Well, what did you come to talk about?' Anna demanded, planting her hands on her hips in case he didn't pick up on her attitude from her tone.

'You!'

The one-word answer echoed around in her head, as if her brain had departed, leaving an empty cavern.

'Me?'

Her fists slid from her hips as uncertainty and hope jostled for supremacy in her heart.

'Yes, you—breaking off your engagement. Penny told me. I'd have come sooner but I've been busy preg-testing a herd of cows on a property a couple of hundred k's north of here. I stayed up there and inseminated the ones who'd failed the first time.'

Anna nodded. It was the kind of information Tom had

often imparted to her in the course of far more normal conversations.

'Anyway, it was stupid. Philip's exactly right for you. You've got to get your act together and tell him you made a mistake.'

'Philip is not exactly right for me!' Anna said, firing the words at him with the snap and velocity of bullets. 'For a start, I don't love him.'

Tom stepped towards her, then, as if yanked backwards by an invisible cord, stepped back again.

'There's more important things than love,' he said firmly, then he ruined the strength of this statement by running his fingers through his hair. 'Especially out here.''

Tom stepped towards her again, close but not touching.

'Look,' he said, 'I know I hurt you that night. It hurt me even more to say no, but I know I'm right, Anna.'

Now he touched her, reaching out and taking her hand, drawing her back towards the house.

'Let me tell you.'

She let him lead her inside and usher her towards one of her lounge chairs. Taking what seemed to be for ever, he settled in the one opposite her.

'My mother was a teacher and she came out to teach in a town not unlike Merriwee. My father was a stock and station agent—you've met some of those guys around town, they organise cattle or grain sales, and handle a lot of other business for the farmers. Anyway, she fell in love with him and he with her and though she was a city girl, she loved the outback and was sure it was where she wanted to spend the rest of her life. My parents were married in the middle of a drought but things got worse and the town was slowly dying. My father said it was the town dying that did it, though I think that's fanciful. What I do know is that when I was three years old, she took a handful of pills and didn't wake up.'

Anna closed her eyes as anguish for the child who'd

probably tried to wake his mother swept over her. She looked in horror at the man who'd been the three-year-old abandoned by a woman for whom the bush had proved too much. She wanted to hold him—and kiss away the pain—to never let him go. But hugs and kisses sometimes weren't enough. Sometimes words were needed as well.

Strong words.

'So on the basis of one woman who might have been depressed before she ever came to the outback—who might have had a history of depression for all we know—you turned me down and now keep telling me garbage about Philip being better for me.'

She folded her arms across her chest and, because thinking about his rejection made her angry, she scowled at him again.

'Your mother might have been suffering from postnatal depression, and probably because the town didn't have a doctor, no one diagnosed it. But, no, you put it down to the killer outback and rule all women not born and bred here out of contention as a marriage partner.'

No, that was wrong.

'What about Grace?' Anna corrected herself. 'She was city-bred. Yet you asked her to come out here. Was she a sponge-cake champ like Bertha?'

Tom raised his hands in surrender.

'I have no idea why sponge cakes keep bobbing up in your conversations but, no, Grace wasn't a country girl but when we got engaged, I was working in a city practice and imagined I'd be there for a long time. It was only when Pat married Keith that I was free to leave, and I believed I knew Grace well enough to think we'd make a go of it anywhere.'

'And you were wrong!' Anna reminded him, and he had to smile at the note of triumph in her voice.

'I was,' he admitted, 'but surely you can understand how

Grace's defection only strengthened my fears about how a woman from the city might fit in out here.'

Anna was about to explode when the phone rang.

'Anna, the baby's on the way and Brian's not here. He went to get Mum. I thought the contractions were just discomfort kind of pains, but now they're too close for me to drive—Aagh!'

The cry of pain interrupted the panic-stricken flow of words, and Anna realised it must be Dani, though she hadn't seen anything of Dani for a while and had assumed she'd gone to Rocky to await the birth of the baby.

'Have you phoned an ambulance?' she asked. 'You'd be better off coming straight to the hospital.'

'I phoned them first,' Dani wailed, 'but it's doing a patient transfer to Deep Springs. It won't be here for an hour, and I'm hurting. Could you come now?'

'I'm on my way,' Anna promised, disturbed by the note of panic in Dani's voice.

She glanced across at Tom, who was standing up, looking uncertainly towards her.

'Dani?' he asked anxiously.

Anna nodded, busy thinking of what she'd need, grabbing her car keys then phoning the hospital to have them get out a baby bundle.

'I'll pick it up at the emergency entrance as I go past,' she told the nurse on duty.

'I'll drive you,' Tom told her, taking the keys from her unresisting fingers.

Anna registered Tom's offer on so many different levels she felt dizzy, but primarily it was relief that someone else would be on hand while she delivered Dani's baby.

Unfortunately, once she was seated in the car beside him, she remembered the downside of being in Tom's company, having to suffer all the physical manifestations of being close to Tom—heat, ice, shakes and shivers.

Yet somehow she kept functioning, directing him back

around through the emergency entrance so she could pick up a made-up bundle that should include everything a new-born baby and the doctor delivering same could possibly require.

He took off like a man out to break a land-speed record, and Anna strapped herself into the seat then clung grimly to the hand-hold above the door. Tom didn't speak, all his attention centred on the road and on getting the speeding vehicle safely out to Dani's place.

He slid to a halt at the gate, and Anna leapt out, opened it and held it, then closed it once the car was through. She smiled to herself as she climbed back into the car, thinking how much she'd learned about the outback since that first, nervous drive with Tom. But the smile faded as she glanced towards him. He was silent, focussed, and, now she knew his deep-held fears about the effect of the outback on women, as unavailable to her as the moon.

Remembering what Tom had said to her about the moon, she muttered, more to herself than to him, 'Philip might have been able to give me the moon, but even his money couldn't buy what I really wanted.'

Tom glanced her way.

'And what was that?' he asked as he pulled up outside Dani's house.

'Love! The kind that lasts and keeps people going through the bad times as well as the good. The kind of love I want to feel for the man I marry and know he feels the same love for me. The kind of love you say isn't enough! Well, that's your opinion!' Anna snapped, climbing out of the vehicle and slamming the door behind her.

Dani was lying on the couch where Anna had first met her, but this time her distress was that of pain, not illness.

'I thought you'd have been in Rocky by now,' Anna said, examining the labouring woman and confirming the baby's arrival was now imminent, though Dani denied feeling anything beyond a mild discomfort prior to the strong contractions starting only an hour earlier.

'Jess said you'd deliver it if I stayed here,' Dani panted. Her brown eyes looked pleadingly into Anna's. 'I was born here, and my mum, and Grandma before her. Probably her mother, too. I wanted the baby born in Merriwee, not in Rocky where no one even knows my name.'

Anna empathised with Dani's feelings about having the baby in Merriwee. In fact, with the FOG on hand for emergencies, she really couldn't see why women couldn't have their babies in Merriwee Hospital. It was something she would have encouraged, if she'd been staying longer...

She sent Tom to find some clean towels and a sheet, checked both the mother and the unborn child, pleased to hear strong foetal heartbeats and see no signs that indicated danger for either the mother or child.

'Are you comfortable on the couch, or would you rather be in bed?'

Dani waited until another contraction passed, then explained she'd tried the bed and the couch was better. Anna spread the towels and sheet underneath her patient then continued her examination.

Dani was four centimetres dilated, the foetal heart rate strong, then suddenly there was a spontaneous rupture of the membranes and Anna was concerned to see the amniotic fluid stained with meconium.

Thinking of the problems this could cause to newborn lungs, Anna crossed to where she'd left her bag and brought out a bag of saline.

'I'm going to flush this into you, so you'll have more fluid sloshing around,' she said to Dani, and though the labouring woman—totally focussed on her pain—took little notice of this remark, Anna knew Tom had guessed there was a complication and had tensed.

'Why?' he whispered, following her to the table and watching as Anna prepared the infusion.

'It will flush out the meconium which presents a danger if the baby breathes it in,' Anna told him, hoping she sounded more confident than she felt. 'Hold this,' she added, handing Tom the bag and tubing while she extracted the foetal scalp monitor, which was part of the bundle, from its packaging.

'I'll attach this to the baby's head to check heart rate variations,' she explained to Tom. 'But Dani probably won't even realise it's there so don't alarm her.'

Tom gave her an 'as if' look and accompanied her back to the patient. At Dani's cry, he settled back down beside her, his arm around her shoulders, urging and encouraging, rubbing at her back with steady hands.

Anna waited until the contraction finished then helped Dani lie back along the couch.

No problems except she was once again sharing a birth scenario with Tom Fleming, and the powerful intimacy of the situation was causing chaos in her mind and body!

She walked away, going back to where she'd spread the baby bundle on the dining table and checking the contents—again—setting aside what she hoped she wouldn't need and spreading a sterile sheet to receive the new arrival.

Checked her patient once more, pleased to see the dilatation continuing, but concern for the unborn child nagged at her. If Dani was at the hospital, would she hurry up the labour? Prepare for a Caesar?

Deciding the answer to both questions was no, Anna settled down to wait, but worry nibbled like mice at the edges of her mind, and every time she looked at Tom, she knew he, too, was concerned.

But with Dani as comfortable as it was possible to be at this stage of labour, Anna had to be content with monitoring and encouraging while her thoughts, eager to avoid focus on the man who sat beside her patient, also watching, waiting and encouraging, flitted off down strange pathways.

If she stayed in Merriwee…

She turned off that path before she strayed too far, and checked the baby's heart rate yet again, then helped Dani move to a more comfortable position, her hands brushing against Tom's arms as they both supported the labouring woman.

No. Much as she knew she'd like to stay, an accidental brush of hands reminded her that living in the same town as Tom for the rest of her life would be a nightmare. Maybe some other outback town might need a doctor…

Another stupid thought! Just about every outback town she'd ever heard of had trouble getting a doctor willing to stay. She'd find another town—that's what she'd do.

And master sponge cakes…

'I need to push,' Dani announced, and, though Anna urged her to wait a little longer, the baby had decided it was ready. The head crowned, Anna watching to see if an episiotomy might be necessary—and relieved for Dani's sake to find it wasn't—then within seconds the head was out.

While Tom held and talked to Dani, Anna suctioned out the baby's mouth, hoping to clear all the dangerous fluid from the upper respiratory tract, then when Dani pushed again, Anna rotated the emerging infant so one shoulder was delivered, then the other, and within seconds the wrinkled morsel of a human being was in her hands.

A tiny boy! He gave a cry, and was turning a satisfactory pink colour as Anna lifted him high for Dani to see. Then, as Tom helped his friend to sit up, Anna clamped and cut the cord, then knelt and put the little boy in Dani's arms. The look of wonderment on Dani's face brought tears to Anna's eyes, and she brushed them away, knowing they were tears for so many things, not just the miracle of a newborn baby.

A gentle hand brushed against her hair and she knew Tom had seen the tears. She glanced his way and needed no translator to understand the messages transmitted by his eyes—messages of wonder, and need.

Messages of love?

Love?

He didn't want her…

Anna turned her attention to her patient, massaging Dani's stomach to help her deliver the afterbirth.

Bright lights shone through the living-room windows, announcing the imminent arrival of the ambulance.

'I don't have to go in it, do I?' Dani pleaded. 'I really hated being in hospital that last time.'

'I'm sorry but, yes, you do,' Anna told her. 'I want to check out the baby and it's easier to do it at the hospital than here.'

Anna hoped she'd spoken calmly enough for Dani to accept this as normal, but the new mother must have had supersensitive hearing.

'There's something wrong with him?' she cried, clasping the baby more tightly to her.

'No, there's nothing wrong, but as a precaution I want to check his respiratory tract and I need a special laryngoscope for it. The one I carry with me is too big for a newborn.'

Anna explained about the fluid that might be lodged below the baby's vocal cords, where ordinary suctioning couldn't reach, and Dani stopped arguing.

The ambulancemen had entered the room, one wheeling a stretcher and the other carrying a baby crib.

Once again Anna accompanied her patients in the ambulance, while Tom drove her car home.

Home! A word so evocative of family, children, love, she found herself brushing fresh tears away.

*   *   *

It was dark by the time Anna, satisfied that both Dani and the baby were all right, returned to her house. As she crossed the hospital yard, she saw a light on in her house, and wondered why she'd had it on when it had been daylight when she'd left.

By now she'd lived in the country long enough to not bother locking her doors, though she did keep her car, with her medical bag inside it, locked. But some undefined memory prompted her to move, not to the door but to the window. Not only was the light on, but her house was occupied. Tom Fleming lay full length on her living-room floor, his hands cupped around something small in the middle of his chest.

The tension of the afternoon exploded inside Anna, and she stormed through the door.

'Well, make yourself right at home, why don't you?' she yelled, then she sank into a chair as Tom sat up and held out his hand, palm outstretched, a tiny greyish bundle of fur now revealed.

'This is why I came over earlier. I left her in the car because you were throwing things when I pulled up, and she had to wait there until I got back.'

He grinned.

'Fortunately for my upholstery, she was in a box!'

He tilted his hand towards Anna, and she reacted quickly, catching the tiny kitten in her hands and peering into the bright blue eyes.

'Oh, you darling,' she whispered.

'I was rather hoping you'd say that,' Tom said, bringing Anna's examination of her new pet to an abrupt halt.

'I was talking about the kitten, not you,' Anna told him, and he smiled at her, weakening every defence she'd ever managed to erect against him.

'Would you say it about me if I asked you to marry me?'

Anna was so dumbfounded she had to put the kitten

down, afraid that if she didn't, she might tighten her grip on it so much she'd strangle the poor thing.

'You came over this afternoon to tell me all the reasons why you couldn't marry me,' she reminded him. 'In fact, you told me I should be marrying Philip. It wasn't so long ago I've forgotten.'

'No, I came over to give you the kitten,' Tom corrected her. 'It was just—'

'If you mention my throwing things again, I'll throw something at you,' Anna warned him, then had to hide a smile as he quickly scooped up the kitten and held it protectively in his hand.

'Anyway,' he continued, 'things changed, didn't they?'

Anna stared at him, mesmerised by two pairs of blue eyes looking earnestly at her.

'When you said what you did about love,' he continued, forcing her to think back through a very confused and tense afternoon. 'About money not being able to buy it. You see, love hadn't come into any of our conversations. You'd offered to have my babies, so I knew you weren't totally repulsed by me, and our kisses were great, so I knew the physical thing was happening, but love?'

He shook his head as if the problem he'd posed was too big for anyone to answer.

'It's such an airy-fairy kind of thing, hard to pin down, this love,' he continued, almost as if thinking aloud. 'But once you put it as plainly as you did, about wanting to love and be loved in return, I knew you'd got it right.'

Tom beamed at her as if she'd made some miraculous discovery, and had imparted it only to him.

'That's what I want, too.'

He shifted so he was squatting in front of her, then handed her the kitten and cupped both his hands around hers.

'Anna Talbot, I love you,' he declared. 'Now and for ever, with all of my heart.'

He was watching her so closely Anna was afraid to react, terrified if she so much as blinked she'd break the spell binding them together.

Then he smiled.

'You do have the right of reply,' he suggested, and she found herself smiling back.

'I can only reply to a question,' she reminded him. 'And as you turned me down when I asked you, you'd better do the asking this time.'

Tom saw the smile in her beautiful eyes and felt his heart lurch with fear that he might not be able to pull this off.

'Are you still available?' he said, excitement, hope and dread vying for control in his mind and body.

Anna smiled.

'I might be,' she said, and he saw the smile turn to teasing laughter in her eyes, while, even as he watched, the tension he'd sensed since she'd returned home seemed to ease from her body.

'Depending on what?' he said, wanting to touch her—hold her—kiss her…

'On why you want me,' she said, and the gleam of laughter was gone from her eyes.

So many reasons, Tom thought. To be his wife, to bear children so his big house rang with noise and laughter, so he could wake every morning with her in bed beside him…

'Because I love you,' he said, surprising himself by the ease with which the essence of all he wanted to say slipped out. 'All other things are nothing beside that, Anna. I want you because I love you—because life without you wouldn't be a life at all.'

Anna set the kitten down on the floor and slid from her chair, right into the strong arms that opened to enclose her. She felt his body shift until she fitted perfectly against him.

The kiss would have lasted longer if the kitten, bored

with the display, hadn't scratched at Anna's leg. They broke apart, and while Tom brought in the special food he'd purchased for it, Anna fixed the two humans a toasted sandwich.

They sat on the couch to eat it, while the kitten curled up and slept on Anna's lap.

'If you do tire of the outback, we'll shift to the city,' Tom promised, nibbling at Anna's ear when the sandwiches were finished. 'Or go and live in South Africa if you'd rather. Or if your parents like Merriwee, we can turn a couple of the bedrooms into a suite of rooms for them, like a private flat, so they could live with us at least part of the year. I don't think I can employ your cousin, but if you hadn't ever got engaged to Philip, he'd have had to fend for himself...'

Anna could hear the remnants of the worry that had made him turn away from her the night on his veranda, but now, knowing the story of his mother's death, she understood. Then she smiled to herself as she wondered just how big Tom's list of problems and possible solutions would grow if she remained silent. Would he start worrying about where to send the children for their secondary schooling—or what university they should attend?

She turned her head, silencing him with a kiss. Silencing any doubt she might have had herself, as the rightness of it warmed her body and love overflowed her soul. Tender hands explored her back, sliding down to cup her buttocks, pressing her close as need grew stronger, until she knew she had to break away or they'd consummate their love on the floor of the hospital residence living room.

'I want to pop over to the hospital and check on Dani and the baby before I go to bed. Why don't you have a shower while I'm away?'

Tom lifted his right arm and sniffed at his armpit.

'Need a shower, do I?' he said, grinning at her in such a way her heart felt it might burst right out of her chest. 'You're getting a bit fussy, woman. Far as I remember, the first time we kissed, we both smelt of horse!'

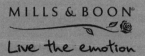

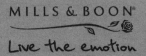

MILLS & BOON®

Live the emotion

Medical Romance™

THE HONOURABLE MIDWIFE by *Lilian Darcy*

A spark of attraction has ignited between GP Pete Croft and midwife Emma Burns. But Pete's ex-wife is ill and his young daughters need him. Emma feels she must do the honourable thing and stand aside. But Emma's generosity simply fires Pete's determination to make her his bride.

THE ITALIAN'S PASSIONATE PROPOSAL
by *Sarah Morgan*

When talented surgeon Carlo Santini rescued Suzannah Wilde one dark, snowy night, the attraction was instant. However, circumstances forced Carlo to hide his true identity. Then he discovered that the new midwife at St Catherine's was Suzannah! How long could his private life remain private when working close together laid bare such strong emotions?

CHRISTMAS IN THE OUTBACK by *Leah Martyn*

Dr Liam Donovan was desperate for a new partner at his Outback practice. Desperate enough to take on his ex-wife! Surely he and Nikki could work together as partners in a strictly *medical* sense? But it wasn't that easy. Soon Nikki and Liam were remembering exactly why they fell in love!

On sale 5th December 2003

Available at most branches of WHSmith, Tesco, Martins, Borders, Eason, Sainsbury's and all good paperback bookshops.

1103/03b

MILLS & BOON

BETTY NEELS

THE
CHRISTMAS COLLECTION

On sale 5th December 2003

Available at most branches of WH Smith, Tesco, Martins, Borders,
Eason, Sainsbury's and all good paperback bookshops.

4 Books

and a surprise gift!

We would like to take this opportunity to thank you for reading this Mills & Boon® book by offering you the chance to take FOUR more specially selected titles from the Medical Romance™ series absolutely FREE! We're also making this offer to introduce you to the benefits of the Reader Service™—

- ★ FREE home delivery
- ★ FREE gifts and competitions
- ★ FREE monthly Newsletter
- ★ Books available before they're in the shops
- ★ Exclusive Reader Service discount

Accepting these FREE books and gift places you under no obligation to buy; you may cancel at any time, even after receiving your free shipment. Simply complete your details below and return the entire page to the address below. *You don't even need a stamp!*

YES! Please send me 4 free Medical Romance books and a surprise gift. I understand that unless you hear from me, I will receive 6 superb new titles every month for just £2.60 each, postage and packing free. I am under no obligation to purchase any books and may cancel my subscription at any time. The free books and gift will be mine to keep in any case.

M3ZEF

Ms/Mrs/Miss/Mr ....Initials...................................
BLOCK CAPITALS PLEASE

Surname..

Address..

....

....Postcode ....

Send this whole page to:
UK: The Reader Service, FREEPOST CN81, Croydon, CR9 3WZ
EIRE: The Reader Service, PO Box 4546, Kilcock, County Kildare (stamp required)